Girl Talk

Renée Kent

ADVENTURES IN MISTY FALLS

7

Girl Talk

Renée Kent

New Hope® Publishers

Birmingham, Alabama

New Hope® Publishers
P.O. Box 12065
Birmingham, AL 35202-2065
www.newhopepubl.com

Library of Congress Cataloging-in-Publication Data

Kent, Renee Holmes, 1955-
  Girl talk / Renee Kent.
      p. cm. — (Adventures in Misty Falls ; bk. 7)
Summary: Over the Thanksgiving holiday, ten-year-old Robyn, who lives
with her aunt and uncle, shares special times with her family and
friends and must adjust to the thought that her body is changing and to
the news that her aunt is expecting a baby.
  ISBN 1-56309-455-X (pbk.)
  [1. Family life—Fiction. 2. Babies—Fiction 3. Friendship—Fiction. 4.
Christian life—Fiction.] I. Title.
  PZ7.K419 Gi 2001
  [Fic]—dc21
                                        00-012388

Cover design by Todd Cotton
Cover illustration by Matt Archambault

Misty Falls, Georgia

Girl Talk

1

Robyn Morgan didn't know who invented book bags, but in her opinion they were the best invention ever. At the current moment, she had a very good, *very heavy* reason for thinking so.

Book bags were right up there on her list of favorites with laptop computers and CD players. Tossing her belongings into a book bag and slipping it on her back left her hands free to wave at friends, open doors, get a drink from the water fountain, and buy a cool pencil in the school store on the way to homeroom. Robyn was always really thankful for her book bag.

But on the morning before Thanksgiving Day, Robyn would have been more thankful if she could have had an *extra* book bag. Although hers was filled to overflowing, it was not nearly big enough to carry all she needed to bring to school. When she awkwardly stepped off the school bus and walked into Misty Falls Elementary School, she was lugging a whole lot more than just her book bag. She had packed it extra full, but she still needed both hands and arms to carry all her Thanksgiving-related stuff.

Rattle, snarf, clunk. Rattle, snarf, clunk. A funny sound seemed to follow Robyn into the school building. For a moment, she stopped in the hallway to catch her breath and to figure out what was making that weird noise as she walked. Instantly, the *rattling, snarfing,* and *clunking* sounds stopped along with her.

She couldn't help but smile. The clatter was coming from the bulky plastic bags looped on her wrists. The bags were so full that they had been swinging like pendulums on a Robyn-sized clock.

She could feel the *rattle, snarf, clunk* noise, too. Each time she took a step, the bag containing Aunt Felicia's garden vegetables for the Thanksgiving feast skit bounced off her left knee, and the other bulging bag slapped her right side. *Whew!* The clothes and trinkets J.J. had let her borrow for the skit were a lot heavier than Robyn had expected!

Thanks to J.J. Graystone's family, Robyn was pretty sure she would be the best-dressed Native American in the whole skit. Surely the kindergarten and first-grade students of Misty Falls Elementary School would think Robyn was a real live Native American attending the Pilgrims' first Thanksgiving feast at Plymouth Rock.

In her left arm, she carried a real Native American cradleboard that snugly held J.J.'s Navajo baby doll.

Leather laces strapped the baby in place. Long, curly lashes framed the dark eyes. The cheeks were round and full, and the baby's lips were curled into a cute little pout. Robyn had jumped at the chance to borrow J.J.'s real Navajo doll and cradleboard for the Thanksgiving skit.

In her right arm, she gripped the two books that wouldn't fit in her book bag. She had borrowed them from the school media center, and they were about the first Thanksgiving celebration. But that wasn't all. She also carried a small, perfectly round pumpkin that weighed exactly two and a half pounds. She knew how much the pumpkin weighed, because she and Uncle Steve had weighed it. They had set it gently on the vegetable scale in the Morgans' base-ment, after Robyn harvested it from her own spot in Aunt Felicia's vegetable garden.

Robyn was extremely pleased that she had grown this handsome, orange pumpkin all by herself. She had watered it daily and talked to it. Occasionally, she even sang to it, when no one was watching. Surely this was why it was so orange, plump, and round. It was a cheerful little pumpkin.

She had big plans for it too. This morning, she was going to give it to Mrs. Russell, her favorite teacher. Mrs. Russell had said earlier in the week that she loved pumpkin pie and wished she had a good cooking pumpkin for the holidays. Robyn had decided right then and there that her teacher would have a pumpkin from her tiny patch in Aunt Felicia's garden.

Robyn couldn't wait to see the look on Mrs. Russell's face. Wouldn't she be surprised by the gift! *Now, if she could just carry it a little further to her classroom . . . .*

She had counted on her aunt to take her to school and help her into class. But for some odd reason, Aunt Felicia had complained that she was not feeling well and asked Robyn if she would mind riding the bus.

In fact, Aunt Felicia had been spending more time lying down lately. For the first time ever, Uncle Steve had made supper last night while Aunt Felicia rested. Robyn hoped her aunt wasn't getting sick. Her stomach couldn't take much more of Uncle Steve's charred mystery casserole.

Since Aunt Felicia couldn't help, Robyn had been counting on her friend Liz to help her carry things from the bus into the school. But Liz wasn't on the bus that morning, so Robyn was on her own with the heavy load.

As students bustled this way and that in the crowded hall, Robyn felt invisible. Nobody was offering to help her. They were all busy hurrying to their lockers and classrooms and talking with friends along the way.

She found it impossible to shift the weight of her load without dropping everything. Suddenly she felt like that little ant she had seen yesterday in the vegetable garden. While tending her pumpkins, she had bitten into a juicy peach, and a tiny piece dropped into the dirt. She watched for a long time as an ant carried it on his back.

The piece of peach had been three times the ant's size. Robyn could tell he struggled to keep his balance so that his little ant family could enjoy a real feast. *Yep,* thought Robyn, *that's just how I feel this morning— like a little ant under a very heavy piece of peach.*

She took a deep breath and pressed forward, past the music room and the media center. She rounded the corner and entered the fifth-grade wing of class-rooms. Instead of going to her homeroom class as usual, she headed straight for Mrs. Russell's room further down the hall.

Because of several Thanksgiving programs today, the school schedule had been changed. It was like a vacation day, only the vacation was being held at school. That's why Robyn was having fifth period first. She didn't try to figure out why, but she could tell that other students and even the teachers were a little confused this morning.

Seeing Mrs. Russell's doorway in the distance gave Robyn hope, but each of her steps became slower and less steady. That pumpkin was starting to feel as though it weighed 25 pounds!

"This just isn't working," Robyn complained aloud, but nobody paid any attention to her. *If only Liz had been on the bus. . . .*

Then she had a stroke of genius. Instead of having a right armload and a left armload, she decided to "stack" her items and carry the whole thing with both arms wrapped around it all. To make sure she didn't lose her grip, she would clasp her hands together at the base of the load.

But trying to balance a perfectly round pumpkin on top of a Navajo doll in a cradleboard was kind of hard to do. She was pretty sure the doll wouldn't mind having a pumpkin on its nose for just a few moments. After all, it wasn't a real baby.

Once the pumpkin was finally balanced on top of the doll in the cradleboard, she slid the library books with her chin between her chest and the pumpkin. It was quite a balancing act, and Robyn now felt qualified to join a circus.

"Now!" sighed Robyn, excitedly. She proceeded to walk toward Mrs. Russell's class, carefully resting her chin on top of the pumpkin as she walked. *Rattle, snarf, clunk. Rattle, snarf, clunk*, sang the bags.

Ahhhh, she thought. *This is working much better.*

Just then, she caught sight of one of the roughest, biggest boys in Misty Falls Elementary School—Spike Thompson—heading her way. His real name was George, but everyone called him Spike because of his haircut. He was barreling down the hall at breakneck speed. As he approached, Robyn froze in place, holding onto her unsteady Thanksgiving collection.

"Out of my way, GIRL!" he said rudely. She held her breath as he sideswiped her shoulder on his way past. Robyn was pretty sure he had done it on purpose.

As the force hit her, her little body lurched to one side. The pumpkin teetered. Then it tottered, like a basketball on the rim of a hoop. Instead of a pumpkin pie, her prize vegetable was about to become a pile of mush on the floor of the school.

If there was any way at all, she wasn't about to let that happen. Robyn danced around the hallway, trying to regain control of her pumpkin. Despite all her efforts, it looked hopeless.

But at the last possible moment, Robyn managed to nab it with her chin and prevent a disaster. She rolled the pumpkin back on top of the doll with her jaw and chin. *Whew, that was close!*

Still, she had a problem. She was growing wearier by the second. *Maybe I should just park my things and myself in the middle of the hallway,* she thought, *until someone comes by to rescue me . . . .*

"Here, let me help you," sounded a familiar voice from behind her. Robyn turned carefully to make sure that the voice really did belong to—yes, it was Liz!

Liz Lawson grinned, showing a mouthful of braces with bright pink rubberbands around her teeth. She took the pumpkin and the library books from Robyn to ease her friend's load. Her green eyes admired the Native American doll in its bed.

"Oh, Robyn," Liz said, "she's beautiful! Is she yours?"

"No, I borrowed her from J.J. Graystone. She's in middle school. Oh, Liz, thank goodness you showed up when you did," said Robyn gratefully, as the girls walked slowly to class. "Thanks to Spike Thompson, I thought I would have to spend my morning cleaning up a busted pumpkin."

Liz grinned. Her true blonde hair, held back off her face with a yellow ribbon on each side, glistened like corn silk. "Sorry I wasn't on the bus to help you carry these things. I had no idea you were bringing this much to school today!"

"Me neither," said Robyn. "I should have brought a laundry basket to carry it in. So why weren't you on the bus?"

Liz sighed and rolled her eyes as she explained. "Thanksgiving problems…I was helping clean the house this morning and missed the bus. Mom is all stressed out about all the food she has to prepare for Thanksgiving tomorrow."

"Oh," said Robyn. "I know how that is. My Aunt Felicia is pretty flustered about the holiday menu, too. And for some reason, she says she is too tired to cook. So did your mom drive you to school?"

"Yes. At first, she wasn't happy that I had missed the bus. But when my little sister spilled her whole bowl of oatmeal, she was glad that I was still at home to help her clean up. Megan is always leaving such a trail of messes. We've been trying to get ready for company tomorrow, but it's a disaster area with a four-year-old around!"

Robyn giggled, as the girls entered Mrs. Russell's room. Sometimes she thought she wanted a little brother or sister, but maybe she wasn't missing so much after all. Besides, she had Uncle Steve and Aunt Felicia all to herself. She kind of liked being the center of attention.

As the girls entered, the teacher looked up from her paperwork. Her kind, brown eyes peered over the tops of her red reading glasses at Robyn's stash. "Goodness gracious, what's all this?" she asked pleasantly.

Robyn made her way to Mrs. Russell's desk at the front corner of the room. Then she let the heavy burdens roll off her into a heap. Tomatoes and onions tumbled out of the bag of vegetables and rolled across the classroom floor.

"Help yourself," Robyn panted. "These vegetables are for our Thanksgiving feast in the play."

"Oh my," said Mrs. Russell, "Are you all right, Robyn?"

For a moment, Robyn couldn't speak. She was too busy catching her breath after her long trek. "Mrs. Russell," she finally exclaimed, "I've never been so glad to see you in my whole life!"

Girl Talk

2

A small crowd of students gathered up the tomatoes and onions and then circled around to see what else Robyn had. It was fun seeing how curious Mrs. Russell was growing about all the things her tiniest fifth-grade student had brought to school. She took off her reading glasses and joined the students at Robyn's side, eagerly awaiting details.

"Thanks for helping me, Liz," said Robyn, taking the pumpkin from her friend. She handed it to her language arts/reading teacher and announced proudly, "Mrs. Russell, this is for you. I grew it in Aunt Felicia's vegetable garden. It's for making your pumpkin pie."

"What a perfectly lovely pumpkin!" exclaimed Mrs. Russell as only she could do. Her voice always rang out dramatically when she talked. She set the pumpkin carefully on her desk and admired it. Robyn was pretty sure Mrs. Russell couldn't have appreciated the gift any more deeply if it had been a diamond bracelet.

Mrs. Russell gave Robyn a hug and said, "With this pumpkin, I will make my husband and my sisters the best pumpkin pie in Misty Falls! Thank you, Miss. Morgan! What a happy Thanksgiving the Russell family will have because you shared your harvest with us."

Robyn beamed. She adored Mrs. Russell almost as much as Nurse Trixie at the New Hope Center.

When Mrs. Russell's eyes fell on the Navajo doll in the cradleboard, she asked, "Oh, tell me, is this precious doll a prop for our skit?"

"Yes." Robyn held up the doll for curious sets of eyes to see. She told them about her visit to the Graystones' apartment the night before. She explained that when J.J. heard about their First Thanksgiving skit, she had invited Robyn and Aunt Felicia to come by her family's apartment to borrow a few things.

"When we arrived," Robyn said, "J.J.'s mother opened a trunk that held all sorts of colorful fabrics and clothes, beads, feathers, and Navajo jewelry that she had saved from her childhood."

"How generous of Ms. Graystone to loan you some of her keepsakes," said Mrs. Russell.

"She sent some extra handmade Navajo jewelry, so that all of us playing the parts of Native Americans in the skit can wear something special." Some of the girls squealed with pleasure. But the girls who were going to play Pilgrims complained, saying things like, "Hey, why didn't the Pilgrim women wear jewelry?"

"Because," said Mrs. Russell, "it was their lifestyle and religious belief to dress modestly and not to bring attention to themselves. Sorry, Pilgrim girls."

As the lucky "Native American" actresses decided which necklaces, rings, and bracelets they would wear, Robyn went on to share how J.J. chose the special necklace for her to wear in the skit. J.J. had tossed her dark, shoulder-length hair, reached into the trunk, and pulled out the long strand of turquoise-blue beads. Robyn pulled it out of the bag and showed her classmates. "She put them around my neck and said, 'This one matches your eyes.' "

As Robyn shared about the doll and beads, she felt like a silly little first-grader during "Show and Tell." But as everyone *oohed* and *aahed* over the borrowed items, her heart danced inside her chest.

"J.J. is right," said Mrs. Russell, who had also been J.J.'s teacher. "Your eyes are the same color of blue as the beads. You will make a beautiful Native American in our skit. Class, let's remember to write a thank-you note to the Graystones for sharing these wonderful things for some of you to wear in our skit today."

"But wait, that's not all!" exclaimed Robyn. She reached into one of the bags and pulled out the carefully folded dress made of real animal skins that Grandmother Teresa Graystone had let her borrow.

Mrs. Russell was obviously pleased. "Tell us about this dress. Is it handmade?" she asked.

"Yes, Grandmother Teresa tanned the hides and made it for J.J. when she was younger. She's grown out of it now," said Robyn. "As J.J. was showing me the beads, Grandmother Teresa disappeared from the room. When she returned, she was holding this dress."

Robyn told the students and Mrs. Russell that Grandmother Teresa couldn't speak much English. But Robyn knew the dress was special by the way she tenderly held it. The way Grandmother's feeble fingers caressed the soft leather material told Robyn this dress was a keepsake of great value. Yet, she was willing to share it. In a heavy Navajo accent, Grandmother Teresa had said, "For Robyn—for school."

Mrs. Russell liked to cry about lots of happy things, and today was no exception. With happy tears in her eyes, the teacher checked her watch and clapped her hands for the students' attention. "Robyn has inspired us for our skit today! We will head to the auditorium now to get ready to present 'The First Thanksgiving.' It's time for our Pilgrims to dress like Pilgrims and our Indians to dress like Indians."

"Native Americans," corrected Robyn. Then her cheeks turned bright red, when she realized she had corrected her own teacher.

"You're exactly right," smiled Mrs. Russell. "Native Americans. Actors and actresses, gather your things and let's quietly head for the auditorium, single file."

In the girls' dressing room beside the auditorium,

Robyn slipped J.J.'s dress over her slender shoulders. The dress was a perfect fit for her ten-year-old frame, even though J.J. had worn it when she was only seven. And just like Cinderella's glass slipper in the fairy tale, a tiny pair of hand-stitched moccasins matching the dress was also a perfect fit for Robyn.

Usually Robyn secretly wished she could be as big as her other friends in fifth grade. She was always a little too tiny, and she appeared younger than her ten years. But today she was glad to be small enough to wear the dress and shoes that Grandmother Teresa had made for J.J. several years ago.

The fringes on the sleeves and at the bottom of the dress swayed with her movements. She swirled about and let the fringes fly. She felt as though she really could have been a Native American at the first Thanksgiving at Plymouth. If only she had J.J.'s bronze skin instead her own pale complexion!

Meanwhile, Liz had dressed in a long, dark gray dress with a white apron. On her head, she placed a little white cap with white ribbon drawstrings. Feathery wisps of blonde hair peeked out from around the cap. She carried a basket of bright red apples that Mrs. Russell had provided.

When the girls saw each other in costume, their faces lit up. Liz was the first to speak. "I wish I could have been a Native American in this skit. I'd love to wear some of the pretty jewelry you brought, Robyn."

"Oh, but Liz, you look pretty even without jewelry," said Robyn. "You really look like a grown-up!"

"I do?" Liz asked, her cheeks blushing pink.

"Yes! I am shaped like a stick. That's why I can wear J.J.'s dress—the one she wore when she was only seven. You are tall and looking older already. I bet I will stay the shape of a toothpick until I am thirty years old!"

"You will not," giggled Liz. "I wish I were as tiny as you. You remind me of Tinkerbell in Peter Pan."

Mrs. Russell called the children on stage to rehearse a song. Then they heard the other children entering the auditorium. Robyn peeked out the edge of the curtain to see what she could see. They were going to have a full house! Lots of parents had come. She could see Aunt Felicia and Uncle Steve...and they had brought J.J.'s Grandmother Teresa too!

Robyn felt butterfly jitters in her stomach as the curtain went up. *The corn!* Did she have her corn to present to the Pilgrims? Oh yes, there it was in the basket. Robyn told herself to settle down. She couldn't wait for the curtain to go up, yet she didn't want it to ever go up.

Her throat felt as dry as a desert. She adjusted the beaded band around her forehead and made sure the feather was sticking up in back, as the curtain arose. There was no turning back now. The Thanksgiving feast was about to begin!

Girl Talk

3

Knowing Grandmother Teresa was in the audience made her stand up a little straighter and feel more like a true Native American. She hoped she was playing her part well.

As the Pilgrims and Indians on stage stood around their first Thanksgiving feast, the Pilgrims sang a song that expressed their thanks to God for the harvest. Then the Pilgrims offered food to their brown-skinned friends, who had helped them plant crops and showed them how to survive in a strange, new land.

After the skit ended, the crowd gave the actors a standing ovation. Cradling the papoose in her arms, Robyn took her bow and winked at Grandmother Teresa, her aunt, and her uncle. Robyn didn't have to wonder if she had looked the part. The smile on Grandmother Teresa's weathered face told her all she needed to know.

Aunt Felicia and Uncle Steve came backstage and gave her a big hug after it was over. "Great job, Pocahontas," teased Uncle Steve.

By midday, Robyn had sung so many Thanksgiving songs, she was blue in the face. Not only had she solved a Thanksgiving crossword puzzle, colored Tom Turkey's tail feathers, and counted the kernels in five cobs of corn in math class, but she had also helped serve apple cider to teachers, students, and parents in the lunchroom.

Now it was finally time for her to eat. The menu was none other than turkey and dressing—what else? Although Robyn had never tasted pumpkin pie before, she thought she should try it, since Mrs. Russell liked it. So she and Liz sampled the cafeteria's pumpkin pie.

Instantly, the girls' noses crinkled in disgust. Liz quickly gulped down her milk, while Robyn declared, "This tastes like wallpaper paste with a dash of cinnamon. *Ich!*" She wiped her tongue off with her napkin.

Liz shook her head, as she wiped off her milk mustache. "I don't know what Mrs. Russell sees in pumpkin pie," she said.

"Me either," agreed Robyn. "Maybe it's an adult food." So the girls decided to just eat the dollop of whipped cream on top and leave it at that.

After lunch, Robyn and Liz reported to their homeroom class. It was time for the fifth-grade students to attend a special Thanksgiving program at the middle school. So, along with their classmates and teachers, the girls tromped across the schoolyard to the Misty Falls Middle School gym.

A banner was unfurled across the length of the gym that read, "What We Are Thankful For." Judging from that title, Robyn assumed the program would be very serious, maybe even a little dull. She didn't expect the fun they were about to have! The creative arts department of the middle school really went all out for the audience.

First, there was a really funny skit by "French Chef" Iggy Potts and his assistant cooks, J.J. Graystone and Cassie Holbrook. Iggy's red curls stuck out around the tall white chef's hat he wore. Robyn laughed herself silly as the trio demonstrated how NOT to prepare and bake a turkey for Thanksgiving dinner.

Iggy was great at playing the role of an absent-minded chef. He started out on the wrong foot, because he couldn't find his recipe card. After tossing everything out of a drawer, he finally pulled out a card. "I have found it!" he announced triumphantly.

Then he cleared his throat and read the card aloud, "If a turkey and a half lays an egg and a half in a day and a half, how long would it take a grasshopper with one wooden leg to kick the seeds out of a dill pickle?"

Iggy fell silent and thought for a moment. Then he yelled, "Oh for heaven's sake, this is not my recipe for turkey and dressing! This is my math homework!"

So he and his assistants set out to prepare Thanksgiving dinner without the recipe. When he pretended to pluck the turkey's feathers, Robyn guessed that he must really have been plucking feathers out of a pillow hidden behind the counter.

They got the steps all mixed up without their recipe, and Chef Iggy made a huge mess before it was over. By the end of the skit, Iggy, J.J., and Cassie were all covered with flour, and the turkey was burned to a crisp. The chef and his assistants ended up making peanut butter and jelly sandwiches for Thanksgiving dinner. Everyone in the audience laughed so hard that tears were rolling down more than a few cheeks.

After the school band played and the choirs sang, students took turns demonstrating their talents. They danced, or read poetry they had written, or shared artwork they had made to express what they were most thankful for during the holiday season.

Then Cassie shared her reason for being thankful. The crowd that had cheered so loudly was quiet enough that Cassie almost didn't need to use a microphone to be heard in the big gymnasium. Then Cassie cleared her throat. "Hi, for those of you who don't know me, my name is Cassie Holbrook," she began shyly. "I'd like to ask my parents and Coach Blevins and my best friend, J.J. Graystone, to come and stand with me."

As they stepped out of the stands to join Cassie at the microphone, she continued, "Earlier this school year, I made some mistakes. I didn't tell the truth, and I even cheated on some of my school assignments. It cost me my spot on the track team, but worse, it caused the people I love and respect most to distrust me. I am really sorry for making those mistakes, and I'm working hard to earn back their trust.

"So the thing I am most thankful for this Thanksgiving is having people in my life who loved me enough to forgive me when I made those mistakes. They wiped the slate clean and gave me a second chance. So I'd like to sing a song to thank them and to thank God for their forgiveness."

Cassie's soprano voice was as clear and crisp as a mountain spring, as beautiful as the song of a bird. But the feeling she put into the song made tears well up in Liz's and Robyn's eyes. Cassie's mother was so moved by the song that she openly cried into several tissues. Afterward, there was a big group hug down on the gym floor, and Cassie was in the middle.

As everyone applauded for Cassie, Robyn said, "You'd love Cassie and J.J. They are great! I wish we could somehow get together, so that you could get to know each other."

"Me too," said Liz. "Thanksgiving weekend is going to be long and boring at my house. Do you think we could all meet somewhere for a soda after Thanksgiving Day?"

Robyn's eyes lit up. She had an idea that was much better than meeting for a soda, but she decided to hold her tongue. She needed to ask Aunt Felicia first.

As they were leaving the gym, they ran smack into Cassie and J.J. To Robyn's surprise, Liz was as tall as Cassie and almost as tall as J.J., even though Liz and Robyn were the same age. Trying not to be the shortest, Robyn tried to stand up as straight she could. But it didn't help much.

"Hey! What's up?" asked Cassie.

Robyn grinned widely. "I was just telling Liz how much fun the two of you are. Cassie, J.J., this is Liz Lawson. We ride the same bus, and we're in Mrs. Russell's class and homeroom together."

"Hi, it's nice to meet you," said J.J. "Do you both have big plans for the Thanksgiving holidays?"

Liz shrugged her shoulders. "I don't know for sure. The way things were going when I left this morning, I don't think I even want to find out! My little sister was making as big of a mess in the kitchen as you two and Iggy were during that funny skit!"

The girls shared a hearty laugh. Then Cassie said, "We're having a big family get-together tomorrow, but then things will be pretty slow all weekend."

J.J. shrugged. "Our Thanksgiving weekends are always a little boring, since it's always just Mom and me. But this year will be better, since we will have Grandmother Teresa with us."

"Just think how tired we're all going to be of eating turkey and dressing," said Cassie. Then she added, "Ooh, imagine how much fun we would have if we could get together on Saturday!"

Liz's and Robyn's mouths fell open as they looked at each other. Then Robyn said, "That's just what we were saying a few minutes ago! That settles it. Don't make any plans for Saturday just yet, girlfriends. I might be calling you later tonight." Then her eyebrows slid up and down as though she had a marvelous idea.

"Sounds interesting," said Cassie, winking at the others. "I'll be home all night! See you all later!"

"It was great meeting you, Liz," said J.J. "Happy Thanksgiving, everybody!"

"Happy Thanksgiving!" sang Robyn and Liz in chorus.

It was easy to imagine how much fun the girls could have together if only Aunt Felicia would agree and let Liz, J.J., and Cassie sleep over on the back porch Saturday night. By then, everyone would be ready to party!

Girl Talk

4

Before leaving school, Robyn folded J.J.'s dress and collected the Navajo jewelry from everyone who had been in her skit. She placed the dress and jewelry carefully back into her bag. Mrs. Russell had given her a box to place her bag and the Navajo doll and cradleboard in.

If at all possible, she wasn't going to take anything else home. So she left her book bag in her locker, dropped the two borrowed Thanksgiving books off at the media center, and gave Aunt Felicia's vegetables away to her teachers. Getting home was much easier than going to school had been!

As soon as the big, heavy front door swung open, Robyn could smell a rich blend of pies and casseroles baking in the oven. She set down her box and followed her nose to the kitchen, breathing in the aroma along the way. When Robyn entered, Aunt Felicia was peeking into the oven. And to Robyn's surprise, Nana Hart was there, helping Aunt Felicia with the baking.

"Mmmm," said Robyn, patting her middle. "Happy Thanksgiving to my tummy!"

Nana Hart laughed aloud as she dried her hands and opened her arms wide for Robyn. Her granddaughter ran into her loving embrace. "Happy Thanksgiving to you, too, dear Robyn. How was school today?"

"Turkey this, turkey that!" teased Robyn. "Thanks, Aunt Felicia, for coming to our skit this morning!"

"You're welcome, baby bird," said her aunt, kissing Robyn's forehead. "It was an excellent program. I was so proud of you!"

"Thanks," Robyn said. "I made sure I brought home the things we borrowed from J.J."

"Great," said Aunt Felicia. "After Thanksgiving, we'll drive over and return them."

Just then, the oven buzzer went off. Aunt Felicia bent over to get the pies out of the oven. When she set them on the windowsill to cool, she put her hands on her hips and stretched her back with a groan. Then she yawned as she stretched some more.

Hmm, that's odd, thought Robyn, as she stared at Aunt Felicia's stomach. *Her usually flat tummy looks round, like a mound of bread dough is stuffed under her shirt. Maybe she has been tasting her cooking too much.* Robyn kept the thought to herself, in case it might

Girl Talk

hurt Aunt Felicia's feelings to say anything. Robyn knew that her aunt always stayed fit and carefully watched the kinds of foods she ate. Maybe Aunt Felicia had decided not to worry about things like weight over the holidays.

"Dear," said Nana gently, "why don't you get your Aunt Felicia a nice glass of milk? She's been standing on her feet all afternoon."

"Okay, Nana, do you want one too?" Robyn asked, reaching for the glasses.

"Yes, let's all have some milk—to go with a bite of pie. Don't you think we should sample it and see if it tastes all right?" Nana asked, winking at Robyn.

Robyn giggled. "Now you sound just like our neighbor, Mrs. Snow," she said, remembering how she and Mrs. Snow had tasted the elderly woman's cobbler pies before the New Hope Fall Festival a few weeks before.

"What kind of pie are we going to have?" Robyn asked, licking her lips. She hoped it was peach.

"Pumpkin," said Nana.

"Oh no," groaned Robyn. "I think I will just have milk and a graham cracker. Thanks anyway." Then she told them about the wallpaper paste pumpkin pie she had at school that day.

As the three sat at the table with their refreshments, Robyn thought it was just as good a time as any to ask about having her friends over on Saturday.

"I'm afraid we will be at Nana and Papa Hart's for the entire Thanksgiving weekend," said Aunt Felicia.

Robyn's face fell. "Oh," she exclaimed.

"Well, why should that matter?" asked Nana Hart. "Your friends are welcome at my house too, you know. We don't live too far outside of Misty Falls...just on over toward Stone Mountain. Why don't your friends come there? Papa Hart and I would love it. And we're planning a little shopping trip to the mall, too. Would that be all right, Felicia?"

Smiling tiredly, Aunt Felicia agreed. "Okay, you may invite your friends. But someone's parents will have to bring them. We can take them home on Sunday."

Robyn's face turned right side up again. Her glow made Aunt Felicia and Nana both laugh.

She dashed right away to phone Liz, Cassie, and J.J. A sleepover at Nana Hart's was an even better idea! Nana and Papa lived in a big sprawling house under the tallest pine trees in Georgia. There were climbing trees, woods to explore, and Aunt Felicia's old college party dresses to play dress-up in.

Liz's mom wanted to talk to Aunt Felicia, to make sure it wasn't an "imposition," whatever that meant. After a bunch of phoning back and forth, it was all finally settled. The Holbrook family was planning a trip to Stone Mountain on Saturday, so they would bring the girls to the Harts' home. Mr. Holbrook talked to Uncle Steve and got the directions.

Now all the girls had to do was wait until Saturday! That was going to be easier said than done.

Just then Papa Hart emerged from the den. Because his hair was sticking up in the back, Robyn knew he had taken one of his naps in front of the TV.

"Do I smell pumpkin pie?" he asked with a hopeful grin.

After Papa Hart had his pie, it became obvious that he had a secret plan. "I'm looking for someone who would be interested in going home with us tonight," he began. "Now who do you suppose would be interested?"

Robyn thought for a moment. "I have no idea," she said, playing along.

"Well now, it's someone who is bigger than a bread box, but not much bigger," he teased.

Robyn frowned playfully. "What would she do for fun, if she went with you?"

Papa pretended to feel hurt. "What do you mean, what would she do for fun? She always has fun at my house. Besides, if that certain someone went home with us tonight, she could attend the Thanksgiving Day parade with Nana and me."

"Hmmm," said Robyn slyly. She tried not to look excited one single bit. She liked staying over at Nana and Papa Hart's house, but she had never gone there without Aunt Felicia and Uncle Steve. She knew it would be fun!

Adventures in Misty Falls

That's when Papa made his offer even more appealing. "Besides, there's a special surprise for her in the backyard."

Robyn was hooked. Aunt Felicia helped her pack her bag for the weekend, and they were off.

"Will you be all right without me?" she asked Aunt Felicia as they hugged good-bye at the car.

"Of course," she said. "Why do you ask?"

"You haven't felt well lately," said Robyn.

"I'm fine and dandy," said Aunt Felicia. "I promise. Now I will see you in the morning after you get back from the parade. All right? Uncle Steve and I will be there for Thanksgiving dinner. Then you know what Uncle Steve and Papa will do, don't you?"

"Yes," said Robyn, nudging Uncle Steve playfully. "They'll watch football games with their eyes closed." Everyone laughed, but no one as loudly as Papa and Uncle Steve.

"Gobble gobble," said Uncle Steve, as he gave his niece a squeeze. "Have fun, kid. See you tomorrow!"

On the way, Robyn sang, "Over the river and through the woods to Grandmother's house we go!" And although Christmas was still a full month away, colorful twinkle lights were beginning to light up Misty Falls and the Atlanta metropolitan area. So Robyn and Nana Hart made a game of counting how many homes and businesses they could spot that were already sparkling with Christmas lights and decorations.

Robyn was glad to have something to keep her mind occupied. It was so exciting knowing that a surprise awaited her in Papa and Nana's backyard, and that she had sleepover plans Saturday! Whatever could the surprise be?

Girl Talk

5

As soon as the car had pulled into the drive-way, Robyn opened the door and scrambled out. "Whoa there, missy! Just where do you think you are going?" asked Papa.

"You know where I'm going," said Robyn, with her hands on her hips. "I'm going to the backyard!"

"Why would you want to go out there? It's dark!" Papa teased. True to form, he took pleasure in keeping Robyn from learning her surprise for as long as he could. He loved keeping her in suspense. He made her wait in the car with Nana, while he went inside for a moment. "Stay here and no peeking until I get back!"

Robyn felt like squealing, and she would have, if it would have made Papa Hart hurry up and show her the surprise. Nana was no help at all. When Robyn asked for clues, she only said, "My lips are sealed."

Finally, Papa came for her and led her to the backyard. Some crickets were singing a

Adventures in Misty Falls

Thanksgiving song in the woods behind the house. A few stars twinkled above, but not enough to see what Robyn's surprise was. It was really dark back there. She couldn't see anything much in the shadows.

"Well," said Papa, "what do you think?"

Robyn was silent for a moment. "Am I supposed to see something?"

"Why, of course, you're supposed to see your surprise. It's right in front of your face."

Robyn giggled. "Oh, Papa, it's too dark out here. Why don't we turn on a light?"

"Oh, that's a good idea!" he exclaimed.

As if by magic, tiny Christmas lights flashed on. For an instant, Robyn's eyes had to adjust, and then she saw—a camping tent, with Christmas lights decorating the entrance!

Robyn gasped and clapped her hands. Then she hugged Papa and Nana, who were chuckling at her reaction. "Could I go inside?" she asked timidly.

"What are you waiting for?" Papa replied.

Robyn crawled into the tent, which smelled like new canvas. It was roomy and marvelous! The twinkle lights made the tent glow with magic. Inside she saw a flashlight, some downy sleeping bags, and even a picnic basket containing snack foods. Best of all, to her delight, there was a screened "moon roof" so that she could see the stars as she lay on her back.

Girl Talk

Now it was time to squeal! "We girls will have so much fun when my friends come to spend the night!" she exclaimed. "Come inside, Papa. Come on, Nana. This is great!"

Nana crawled in first, then Papa, who sounded like an old bear growling as he complained of his arthritis. The tent was comfortable for all three of them to be inside. They lay down together and looked out the moon roof and made a wish on a blinking star.

"I wish that I could sleep in my new tent tonight," Robyn announced. Then she looked at her grandparents and added, "I don't want to wait until my friends come on Saturday. Could we sleep out here tonight? Please?"

Nana shivered. "I don't know, dear. There's a chill in the air. What do you think, Papa?"

"Of course we can sleep out here in the new tent," said Papa. "Let's go inside first and get on our warm pajamas and brush our teeth, and then we'll meet back out here. What do you say?"

In the glow of twinkle lights around the tent entrance, Nana examined the wistful faces before her. Then she laughed. "Oh, all right. I'm in. Let's go get ready to camp!"

Nana made sure that Robyn was so well dressed that she was actually hot as she re-entered the tent. Not only was she in her pajamas, but over those she wore one of Papa Hart's quilted flannel shirts, which came down to her ankles. Papa Hart wore quilted flannel shirts when he went out to gather firewood in January.

Her feet had on not one, not two, but three pairs of socks. Nana had wanted Robyn to wear a scarf on her head, but Robyn refused. "Nana, it's not snowing!" she'd said. "I'm going to start running a fever if you make me wear any more clothes." And that settled the matter.

As soon as the three had nestled into their sleeping bags, Papa asked, "What have we got to eat?"

Nana and Robyn laughed. "You don't need anything to eat," Nana said, poking his belly.

"Party pooper," said Papa good-naturedly.

"Tell us a story from when you were a boy," said Robyn. He told the best stories in the whole world—stories about camping in the woods with his scout troop, leftover bacon on a skillet outside the tent, and a hungry visiting bear...but just as the story really got interesting—and funny—Papa got very sleepy. His voice trailed off, and his words didn't make any sense.

"Papa, what happened next?" asked Robyn, wide-eyed in the shadows of the tent.

For a moment, there was silence. Then came the soft snores of a very tired grandpa.

Nana and Robyn giggled. Then, as Papa's snores grew louder, Nana said, "I guess the bear gobbled up that bacon and wandered back into the woods, but we may never know for sure."

"I wish we could adjust the volume on Papa like we can adjust the volume on TV," whispered Robyn. "It's too loud to sleep out here, Nana."

The two tucked a blanket over Papa. Then as quietly as they could, they slipped out of the tent, leaving him out there to snore to his heart's content with the night sounds.

For some reason, tiptoeing inside to Nana and Papa's warm bed to sleep in peace gave Robyn the silly giggles. Nana soon joined in. They tried to imagine Papa's look of surprise in the morning, when he would awaken and realize he had been abandoned!

Suddenly, Robyn had a thought and stopped laughing. "You don't suppose a bear will wander out of the woods and get Papa, do you?" she asked.

"There are no bears around here, except in the zoo," said Nana. "Papa is perfectly safe."

"Oh good," said Robyn, lying back on her pillow.

"Oh Miss Robyn, you are a doodlebug," said Nana affectionately. "You know, this is going to the best Thanksgiving our family has had in years."

Robyn thought for a moment. This was the first holiday that she had been able to celebrate with her family outside of a hospital or the New Hope Center in the longest time. The thought gave Robyn a rush of warm tingles all over her body. As she drifted into a fanciful dream containing friends, a tent, and twinkle lights, she whispered, "Thank You, dear God, for making me well." Yes indeed. Perhaps this would be the best Thanksgiving ever.

The holiday certainly started earlier and more loudly than Robyn expected. One minute, she was snuggled peacefully under the covers sound asleep. The next, Papa was standing over her, blaring a very flat tune on his tarnished boyhood bugle.

Wasting no time, Papa, Nana, and Robyn got ready and went into town. They chose a good spot on the Thanksgiving Day Parade route, just as the drum cadence sounded from around the corner. Robyn marched in place on the curb as the snappy band dressed in white, gold, and black strutted by playing their woodwinds and brass instruments. Some cheer-leaders on a float following the band threw wrapped candy to the crowds, and Robyn caught three pieces! She shared two pieces with Papa and Nana and popped the third piece into her mouth.

Next, horses with shiny coats and showy harnesses pranced down the street. To Robyn's surprise, there was J.J. riding her mare, Gracie, in the parade! She wore a smart, black, western hat and a candy-apple red outfit, which matched the saddle blanket and the fluttering ribbons that had been braided into Gracie's mane.

Girl Talk

"J.J.! J.J.! Hi!" yelled Robyn as loudly as she could. She jumped up and down to make sure J.J. found her.

J.J. heard her name, searched the crowd, and smiled brightly at Robyn. With a wave, she called back, "See you Saturday!"

As the horses clip-clopped down the street, swishing their magnificent tails, Robyn watched wistfully. She felt extremely proud to have a friend riding her horse in the parade. How fun it would have been if she, too, could have ridden a horse in the parade. Perhaps one day she would.

Robyn secretly wished something else. More than anything, she wished she could look and be as grown up as J.J. In fact, Robyn had always seemed to grow at a much slower pace than her friends. At this rate, she would never catch up with any of them!

Girl Talk

6

As soon as the parade had ended, Nana was ready to get home to peek in at the Thanksgiving turkey, which had been basting itself slowly in the oven. Papa smacked his lips together and winked at Nana as he put the car in park. Then he said, "First dibs on the turkey legs—one for me and one for Robyn."

Uncle Steve and Aunt Felicia pulled in right behind Papa's car. Robyn tumbled out and ran back to greet them. "Happy Thanksgiving!" she called cheerfully.

Robyn grabbed a sack out of the floorboard and followed Uncle Steve, who hauled a big box full of casseroles and pies to the kitchen. On the way inside, she pointed to her surprise in the backyard.

"See my new camping tent? Won't my friends like sleeping over in such a great tent? It has twinkle lights and everything!" Robyn announced.

"I see! It's wonderful," said Aunt Felicia. Then she added, "Oh, Mom, I'm afraid you and Pops are spoiling Robyn!"

"Oh, my dear," said Nana, exchanging a knowing look with her granddaughter. "That's what grandparents are for! You might as well get used to it, Felicia."

Aunt Felicia pretended to disapprove, but Robyn could tell she was just teasing. While the three women finished putting the final touches on dinner, the men went to see about their televised football game in progress, but not without a promise from Papa.

He called over his shoulder as he clicked on the TV with the remote, "Steve and I will wash dishes later."

"You've got yourself a deal, Pops," Aunt Felicia hollered back from the kitchen sink.

"How are you feeling today, dear?" asked Nana, glancing at her daughter with concern. "You look a little pale."

"Better today," said Aunt Felicia.

Robyn's forehead crinkled. "What's wrong, Aunt Felicia? You've been tired a lot. Have you been sick?"

"No, darling, I'm not ill," said her aunt. "Would you like to set the table for Nana?"

Robyn sighed. Aunt Felicia was good at changing the subject. Into the dining room she went with plates and Nana's best linen napkins to set around the table. She opened the drawer of flatware and began to arrange forks, spoons, and knives beside the plates.

Girl Talk

As she worked, she could hear Nana and Aunt
Felicia talking softly. Robyn had more than just a feeling lately that they were hiding something from her.
Something important. *But why?* She was starting to
feel very jittery.

The last time they had spoken in whispers like this,
it was because Robyn was going to have to go to the
hospital for surgery, but that was a long time ago.
What could this new secret be? She hoped Aunt
Felicia wasn't going to have to go to the hospital.

Well, if they wouldn't tell her what was going on,
Robyn would find out some other way. As the two
women worked over a crystal bowl of homemade
cranberry sauce and a pan of Nana's famous potato
rolls, Robyn tiptoed to the entrance of the kitchen.
She strained to eavesdrop on their conversation. But
she could only make out a word here and there...not
enough to figure out what they were discussing.
Besides, Papa Hart's football game on TV was too
much of a crowd-roaring, whistle-blowing distraction!

She frowned. Why did everybody treat her as
though she were a mere child? She was ten years
old—practically a teenager! And she was very smart
and responsible. If something were wrong with Aunt
Felicia, she needed to know about it. She was old
enough to be of help, after all.

Before long, Nana announced, "Dinner is served."
Papa and Uncle Steve followed their noses to the

dinner table like two hungry, old bears. On his way past the platter of sliced turkey, Uncle Steve sneaked a bite when no one was looking. No one but Robyn, that is.

Robyn grinned as Uncle Steve put his finger to his mouth as if to say, "Shhh—don't tell on me." Robyn zipped her mouth closed and threw away the pretend key. Her lips were sealed!

"Our Father," prayed Papa Hart, as everyone held hands around the feast, "we surely are grateful for all You have done for us. On this day that is set aside to give thanks, we realize how much we have to be thankful for. Thank You for making our Robyn well this past year. We thank You for each person around this table, and for those to come. We thank You for the food we're about to enjoy and for the sweet hands that prepared it. Most of all, we thank You for Your Son, Jesus Christ, who has opened the way for us to live with You for all eternity. We thank You, Lord, for all this. Amen."

As everyone sat down, Robyn was curious about Papa's prayer. He had prayed for each person around the table and *"for those to come."*

"Are there more people coming to Thanksgiving dinner?" asked Robyn.

"No, dear," said Nana, "just us—why do you ask?"

"Papa prayed for the people at our table and 'for those to come.' Did you mean Cassie, J.J., and Liz?

They're coming on Saturday."

Everyone except Robyn chuckled. *What is so funny?* Robyn thought to herself.

Nana smiled warmly at her. "That is what Papa meant," she said, as she passed the sweet potatoes to Uncle Steve. "Now watch out, because this dish is really hot!"

In between the oohing and aahing over the delicious meal, Robyn noticed something strange. Not only were Nana and Aunt Felicia talking in code; even Uncle Steve and Papa Hart were doing it too!

For instance, when Aunt Felicia said something about a due date, Robyn was pretty sure she was talking about library books. They had a whole stack of books at home that had to be returned to the library next week. But then Uncle Steve said the due date had to do with cookies popping out of an oven. Then Papa and Nana laughed, and Aunt Felicia blushed a pretty pink.

It was as though everybody knew the answer to a riddle except Robyn. They seemed to be having way too much fun keeping this secret.

So while Nana and Papa served pie and cake to everyone for dessert, Robyn decided to get to the bottom of this. To make sure everyone paid attention to her, she stood up and put her hands on her hips, for effect.

"Okay," she said with her jaw set and her blue eyes stern. "I have just about lost my patience with you all." Four surprised sets of eyes looked at her.

"Why, what's wrong, baby bird?" asked Aunt Felicia, startled by Robyn's tone.

"Isn't it obvious?" asked Robyn. "You've all been whispering and talking in half sentences and riddles long enough. All of you are keeping something a secret. I am a member of this family, and I should be told what it is. So who is going to tell me?"

Astonished, Aunt Felicia looked at Uncle Steve. Uncle Steve looked at Nana. Nana looked at Papa Hart, and Papa looked at his plate of pumpkin pie and apple stack cake. Robyn wasn't budging until somebody talked. "Well?" she asked.

Everyone looked at Robyn. Finally, they were starting to show signs of taking her seriously! *It's about time*, thought Robyn.

Aunt Felicia held out her arms. "Come here, sweetie," she said. "I do see your point. It's not that we were trying to hide anything from you. We were just waiting a while to tell you."

"Tell me what?" asked Robyn as she drew close to Aunt Felicia.

"That, uh—you're going to be a big sister."

"A—sister?" asked Robyn. She was astounded. Why hadn't she thought of it before? Now it made sense why Aunt Felicia had been resting so much, and why her tummy poked out like a little mound of bread dough. That wasn't from holiday eating—that was a baby in there!

With her mouth gaping open, Robyn looked intently into Aunt Felicia's moist, brown eyes. "Isn't it amazing?" Aunt Felicia said, lovingly patting her tummy.

Well, there it was. The mystery had been solved. Only now, she had a million and one questions. But "oh" was all Robyn could manage to say.

For a moment that seemed to last an hour, all was silent around Papa and Nana Hart's dining room table. Robyn looked at each of them. Was this true? The round little heap under Aunt Felicia's blouse told her it was. She was going to be a big sister...or wait a minute! Was she?

All of a sudden, Robyn remembered that her own parents were in heaven. Although she thought of Aunt Felicia and Uncle Steve as her real parents now, they really were her aunt and uncle. But now that their own baby was coming along, perhaps they wouldn't need or want Robyn anymore. . . .

Girl Talk

7

Robyn took a step away from Aunt Felicia. "You're going to be a mother," said Robyn quietly. "And Uncle Steve will be a dad. But you are my aunt, and Uncle Steve is my uncle. Let's see...that means I am not going to be a sister at all. I am going to be this baby's cousin!"

"See, Mother? I told you this might happen," muttered Aunt Felicia to Nana. She seemed to sense Robyn's worries.

Then Aunt Felicia turned her full attention to Robyn. Tiny tears glistened in her soft eyes. She said, "Now dear one, sit down with me a moment. Yes, biologically, you were born to my sister. But a long time ago, Steve and I adopted you to be our own, and we will never change our minds about that. You are our first child. This baby that is growing inside me is our second child. That's why you should think of this baby as your little brother or sister, not your cousin. Do you understand?"

"I think so," said Robyn with a smile, relieved to know that she was still Aunt Felicia's "baby bird." Then her forehead crinkled, which made her up-turned nose curl up a little higher. "So did your Thanksgiving meal fall down on top of the baby?"

Nana and Papa laughed loud and hard at that. Aunt Felicia smiled, and replied, "I'm so full that it feels like it!" Then she explained there was a separate place for babies to grow inside a woman's body—a place called the womb.

"It's a warm, wet place that only females have," said Nana, winking at Robyn, "just right for growing babies."

"It's wet in there?" asked Robyn. "I hope the baby can swim! Hey, I'm a female. Do I have a womb too?"

"God is preparing a womb inside your body, for when you grow up and become a wife and mother," said Aunt Felicia.

That's when Robyn said, "Ich! I don't ever want a baby, thank you! I don't think there would be enough room inside me to grow a whole baby."

Then there was another round of laughter, before Robyn asked more questions. . . "Is it a boy or a girl?" (Aunt Felicia didn't know yet.) "Will the baby have teeth?" (No, teeth come later.) "When will the baby be born?" (Not for a few more months.) "How did the baby get in Aunt Felicia's womb in the first place?" (We can discuss that later.) "How will it get out? Why isn't this a good question to ask right after

Thanksgiving dinner?"

Robyn was getting cranked up with her question-asking, when Uncle Steve exclaimed, "Whoa, hold your horses! One question at a time. In fact, Papa Hart, maybe this is a good time for you and me to go wash dishes and let these ladies have a private talk."

As Uncle Steve and Papa happily excused themselves from the table, Nana laughed and said, "I've never seen two grown men look so delighted to leave the dinner table and wash dishes in my life!"

Robyn turned to Nana and Aunt Felicia. With a frown, she asked them one final, crowning question that capped them all. "Why am I the last to know about this baby stuff anyway?"

"There now," said Aunt Felicia, "we have plenty of time to get used to the idea. The baby will not be due until late February or early March. So you see, that's why Uncle Steve and I were not in a hurry to tell you the news. We have been adjusting to the idea ourselves!"

"Oh," said Robyn. She supposed that made sense. "But how did you know you were going to have a baby?"

"Well," said Aunt Felicia. It was pretty obvious that she didn't know how to broach the subject with Robyn. "You remember what happens each month that a lady isn't going to have a baby. The body gets rid of the extra fluids that would have been reserved if a baby was present in the womb."

"Oh yes," said Robyn, "a menstrual period." She had read a book with Aunt Felicia explaining what happens. It sounded pretty messy, in Robyn's opinion. But her aunt had said it was actually a beautiful plan that God had in place for women and their families.

"Well, when I missed a menstrual period, and then another, I went to the doctor. He said a baby was growing inside me," she said happily. "I'm going to the doctor for a checkup next week. Would you like to come? Perhaps you could hear the baby's heartbeat!"

"Okay," said Robyn sullenly.

Then she noticed the anxious look on Aunt Felicia's face. Although her aunt was smiling, she also looked as though she might burst into tears any moment.

Nana Hart patted Robyn's shoulder. "Won't we have fun with the new baby? What a precious gift from God!"

Robyn wasn't so sure. *Did she really have to be thankful for this news?* Not that babies weren't special. They were just kind of noisy and messy like Liz's little sister, who had spilled oatmeal that Liz had to clean up. Robyn was pretty sure that a warm, wiggly puppy would be much more fun.

Still, she didn't want to upset Aunt Felicia by not accepting the news. So she said, "You will be a wonderful mama, Aunt Felicia. And I will help." And with that, Robyn gave her aunt a kiss on the cheek, even though she didn't feel much like being a big sister at all.

Girl Talk

8

By Friday, Robyn was bored stiff and ready to be adventurous. But there was nothing much to do but mope around. She wished it were Saturday, so that her friends could come over. She needed to talk to J.J., Cassie, and Liz. They would understand why she wasn't excited about the new baby. At least, she hoped they would.

It seemed that all Aunt Felicia wanted to do was take naps. And Nana had started knitting a baby blanket. So neither of them was available to do the special things that Robyn wanted to do—climb trees, go for long walks in the woods, or play Pass the Pigs, checkers, or Concentration.

After playing herself in checkers, Robyn sighed. Nana, who was curled up in her easy chair with her yellow yarn, didn't seem to care that Robyn was bored. So she decided to slip off to her tent.

Nana's place contained every kind of flowering bush known to Georgia in the yard and gardens. By using her imagination, the weeping willows, camellias, and English ivy became heavy vines and undergrowth in Africa. She pretended to be in the dark recesses of a jungle where there were no babies, except baby tigers, of course.

Just as her adventure was getting interesting, Papa Hart peeked into the tent. "Come on, my little African Queenie! Let's go for a ride."

"Where are we going?" Robyn asked, but she didn't wait for the answer. She sped past Uncle Steve and Papa to the pickup truck. She always loved going for rides, especially with her two favorite fellas.

"My dear, we are going to scale one of the biggest chunks of solid granite rock east of the Mississippi River," he said, turning on the engine and shifting the gears. "I hope you have your walking shoes on!"

"I do!" said Robyn, lifting her feet to show him. "Oh goodie! We're going to Stone Mountain!"

While lying in hospital beds recovering from her injuries, one of her dreams had been to someday climb Stone Mountain. As she recovered from her accident, she had been able to see the gray rock mound rising above the city from her hospital window. It had seemed to Robyn that Stone Mountain was God's special contribution to Atlanta's city skyline.

On a long-ago Sunday afternoon picnic at the base of the mountain, she had sat in her wheelchair, looking up at the tiny people on the pinnacle. Their ability to climb the mountain made her long to trek up the mountain trail too, but she had not been physically able to hike then. Now she would finally get her chance!

As she sprang from the truck and skipped across the parking lot, Robyn sang, "That's the biggest chunk of rock I've ever seen. Come on, Uncle Steve, I'll race you!"

Unleashing lots of pent-up energy (and baby blues), Robyn sped ahead of her uncle and Papa. With each step, she was a little more pleased that her legs were so strong now. She felt that she was capable of running all the way up the mountain if she wanted. It was a wonderful feeling that had been worth waiting for!

Of course, that's how Robyn felt along the bottom third of the trail. By the time they had climbed about halfway, her pace had slowed down quite a bit. A little breathless now, she didn't talk to quite as many hikers who were making their way down the mountain trail. So she put her head down and her legs to the task. She *was* going to make it, even if her legs ached until Christmas.

Papa Hart called out from behind her and Uncle Steve. "Whew! Would you look at those trees... I wonder what kind of tree that is?"

Robyn turned to look. It was just a plain old everyday Georgia pine tree. She was getting ready to say so, when she realized what Papa was doing. He was pretending to "admire the scenery" so that he could catch his breath! Robyn laughed and ran back to him to give him a hug.

"That is a beautiful Georgia pine tree," said Robyn. "Silly Papa, come on. We're going to finish this!"

"Do we have to?" asked Papa. "I think I'll sit down under this pine tree and take a nap. You can wake me when you come back down."

Giggling, Robyn got behind Papa and pushed him up with her arms. "Oh no, you don't! I'm not giving up, and you aren't either! We're going to crawl the rest of the way if we have to!"

"She might be little, but she's tough," said Papa to Uncle Steve.

Almost to the top, Robyn caught her second wind and began to feel stronger again. The air was a little cooler and the sun a little brighter, without the shade of the tree line. With Uncle Steve on one side and Papa on the other, Robyn finished her triumphant climb.

One-two-three-HOP! Robyn had officially made it! "TA-DA!" she sang. The brisk air in her lungs made her feel as light as a balloon. She held tightly to Papa's jacket, as they walked around on top of the rock, in case the wind might sweep in and blow her right off the mountain.

At first the cold gray surface at the top of Stone Mountain looked as lifeless as pictures of the moon, which Robyn had seen in magazines and books.

Uncle Steve pointed out places where rain puddles had carved out smooth dips in the rock over the years.

Then Robyn noticed that the top of this rock wasn't lifeless at all. From the cracks and crevices of the rock mountain, tiny wildflowers and grasses captured sun-rays. She wondered if butterflies flew up this high for nectar in the summertime. She would have to come back and find out.

They sat down carefully on the smooth, hard crest of the mountain and let their legs dangle over the side. Robyn was glad there was a safety fence a few yards below, just in case she were to lose her balance. Resting on her bottom felt safer than standing. Besides, it felt good to take a breather after the long climb!

The city sprawled out before them for as far as she could see. As she had heard Papa Hart say often, he began to muse over how much Atlanta had grown since he was a boy. "I remember when that hotel with the blue dome restaurant on top was the tallest build-ing in the city. Now look! You can hardly see it for the skyscrapers around it! I declare, I don't know how they're going to put one more building or person in this area."

Robyn interrupted. "Where is Misty Falls? Can we see it from here?"

Papa looked northwest and pointed. "Way out

there—see that patch of woods beyond Kennesaw Mountain?"

Robyn wasn't sure she had the right mountain in view. There were lots of smallish mountains that looked more like hills compared to what she was sitting on! "I think so," she said.

"See the mist rising above the trees—there?" added Uncle Steve.

"Yes!" said Robyn. "Is that where the Misty Falls waterfall is?"

"You're exactly right," he replied. "Our house is tucked underneath those trees just to the left of where you see mist rising."

From where she sat, Misty Falls was the size of a very small pebble she had found in her shoe along the trail. Suddenly, she felt as tiny as a speck of dirt— a microscopic speck at that!

"Can we see the whole state of Georgia from up here?" asked Robyn.

"Oh no, Georgia is much bigger than what we can see," said Papa.

"Wow! Then God is much bigger than I thought He was," said Robyn. She tried to imagine how big the whole state was—then the whole country. Then how really big the earth must be. Then how vast the whole universe was, with all the stars and planets and space. She could not even begin to imagine it all! God had to be very powerful and wise and creative to make all this...and heaven too!

Papa chuckled. "To the good Lord, Stone Mountain must be about the right size to pick up off the ground and skip across the Atlantic Ocean."

"He won't do that with us sitting on it, will He?" asked Robyn, whose imagination was always running at full speed.

"No, I think He likes Stone Mountain right where He put it," said Uncle Steve.

"And He likes you just where He put you, squirt," added Papa, tweaking her tummy.

"Hey, Pops," said Uncle Steve, "did I ever tell you that I brought Felicia up here and asked her to marry me almost nine years ago? I'm sure glad she said yes." From the soft look in Uncle Steve's eyes, Robyn could tell that he loved Aunt Felicia as much as ever.

"And now, here you are, expecting your firstborn baby," said Papa with a smile.

Until then, Robyn had pleasantly forgotten about the big Thanksgiving news. She sighed. *Why couldn't she be happy about the baby?* She had always liked little children. After all, she had been a big sister to many of the patients at New Hope Center, especially Maddie Harris, Hunter's little sister. She was good at throwing tea parties for Maddie and her dolls in their secret hiding place under the bushes at New Hope Center.

But now that this was going to happen, she felt

unsettled. Of course, she was curious to see the baby and felt happy for Aunt Felicia and Uncle Steve, but she couldn't shake the feeling that somehow she was being replaced. Things would never be the same again.

Robyn tried to shake off the ill feeling. She wanted to remain as carefree as she had been on her hike, but even Papa and Uncle Steve noticed the instant change in her mood. That's why Robyn was no good at playing Old Maid and other games where she had to bluff her opponent. To her own dismay, her face told all!

"Hey," said Uncle Steve, nudging her with his elbow. "Why the long face?"

Robyn managed a grin. "I guess I'm still getting used to the idea of a baby in the house."

"Whew!" exclaimed Uncle Steve. "You can say that again."

"You mean, you feel the same way?"

"Sure," said Uncle Steve. "I admit that I am a little nervous. A baby who totally depends on you for everything—wow. That's going to be a lot of responsibility. But it will be fun, too."

Robyn wasn't so sure, and Papa could tell. He put his arm around her and told the story of the first time he ever saw Robyn. "It was in the hospital right after you were born. The nurse held you up, all pink and wrinkled."

Girl Talk

Robyn laughed, trying to imagine herself as a tiny baby. Papa continued, "You were wrapped up tight in a pink and blue blanket, and you had a little curl flipping out from underneath a snug little cap. Your fingers were long and slender, and your tiny little nose turned up just the way it does now. Suddenly, I realized, 'I'm a grandfather!' and that changed my life. My heart has been wrapped around your little finger ever since."

Papa Hart always knew just what to say to make Robyn feel better. At least she knew if Aunt Felicia and Uncle Steve got too busy with the baby, she would always have Papa's heart.

Still, she wanted to find a way to accept the baby news with joy, like Aunt Felicia had. She was sure that everyone wanted her to be glad about the baby coming. But now that she was ten, going on eleven, she had more interesting things to do with her time than being up to her eyeballs in diapers and baby bottles. She was practically a young lady! Now was her time to really live!

On the way back down the mountain, Papa listened as Uncle Steve explained his chief concern about the baby's arrival. "The more I learn about how much it costs to have a baby this day and age, the more nervous I'm getting," he said. "I just don't know how Felicia and I are going to make ends meet."

"Don't worry, son," said Papa. "Financial worries are temporary. They don't last forever. How do you climb any mountain?"

"One step at a time?" Robyn guessed.

"Exactly right," said Papa. "Sometimes we might stumble over a tree root, or we get tired, and we can't see the point anymore of finishing the hike. Sometimes we might rather give up."

"Yeah, remember Papa, you wanted to stop and take a nap under the pine tree, but you would have missed that beautiful view at the top of Stone Mountain!" exclaimed Robyn.

"Yes, I would have missed it all right," said Papa. "You were here to encourage me to keep going, Robyn. And God gave us all the strength to finish our journey to the top together."

"What has that got to do with Uncle Steve worrying about money?" asked Robyn.

"Oh, well, I was just going to say that money worries don't last. It's families sticking together through the temporary troubles that matter. You'll make it, one step at a time, and in the end, you'll see beautiful results," said Papa. "Just be patient, son, and do your best to thank God every step of the way, even when the going gets tough."

Robyn thought for a long while with her mouth twisted up. "Are you trying to tell Uncle Steve and me we should be thankful for babies that cost a lot of money and mess up our fun?"

Uncle Steve exploded in laughter and put his arm around Robyn's shoulders. "Not exactly! I think I know what Papa means. He is reminding us that God has blessed our family. He wants me to be a dad, and He wants you to be a big sister. This is a special honor. So we need to have a thankful attitude about this baby, and God will provide a way for us to enjoy His blessing."

"Did I mean all that?" Papa asked. Then he joked, "I'm wiser than I thought!"

Robyn thought silently. It was strangely comforting to hear Uncle Steve, who didn't like to go to church with Robyn and Aunt Felicia, talking about God and being thankful. And it was true that God's Word said to give thanks in all things.

Maybe God would help her become a good big sister in time. Maybe she would learn to love the baby and her new role as big sister. Still, she couldn't imagine herself helping take care of a baby, day in and day out.

So right then and there, she decided that she had better pray. "Thank You, God, for this baby, I think. But Uncle Steve and I are going to need all the help we can get. Amen."

Girl Talk

9

One thing was certain. It was much easier walking down a mountain than walking up. In no time at all, they had arrived at the truck, and Robyn was terribly thirsty. They stopped by a soft drink stand and headed home. Orange soda rushing down her dry throat tasted awfully good!

When they arrived home, her legs did ache as she climbed out of the truck cab. But it was a good sort of ache. Her muscles had been really challenged, but they had passed the test. Robyn couldn't wait to go inside and tell Nana and Aunt Felicia about climbing Stone Mountain—on her own two legs!

On the way into the house, she thought she heard a noise from the backyard. Was that a fussy squirrel, or had someone just giggled? Robyn listened.

There it went again. A low buzzing noise, and then "Shhh!" Robyn ran to the backyard to check it out. No one was in sight, not even a squirrel or a bird.

Just as she was about to go inside, she noticed that there was something different about her tent. When she had left with Papa and Uncle Steve, she was sure she had left the door flap unzipped. Now, it was zipped closed. Maybe Nana had closed it for her.

She bent down to unzip the opening. Even though she tried her hardest, the zipper wouldn't budge. Up, down, up, down. Over and over, Robyn tried to get the zipper unstuck, without success.

Finally, she decided to call for Papa to come and help her. But just as she was about to yell for him, she heard a chorus of giggles coming from inside the tent. Then the zipper started working—all by itself, it seemed!

Robyn peeked into the tent to see Cassie, J.J., and Liz surrounded by their sleeping bags and pillows. "Surprise!" they exclaimed.

It took a moment for Robyn to find her voice. "Aren't you here a day early?"

"Yes," said Cassie. "That's the surprise, silly!"

"Your grandmother called and said you were bored," explained J.J. "We would have been here earlier, but Cass and I had to wait for the large animal veterinarian to come and visit Chester and Gracie. It was time for their equine vaccinations."

Liz grinned. "So are you glad we came early?"

Robyn beamed hopefully. "Can you still stay until Sunday?"

Girl Talk

"Yes," sang the girls. Then they giggled at themselves.

"Then it's party time! We'll have lots more girl time this way," said Robyn, jumping up and down. "Scoot over. I'm coming in!"

"I love your tent," said J.J. "Your Nana said we could sleep out here. I'm so excited! I haven't been camping in such a long time."

"I've never been camping," said Liz. "This will be my first time."

"It's a blast," said Cassie. "You'll love it. There's nothing like waking up to the fresh air of the outdoors."

"I hope you all brought warm pajamas," said Robyn. "Otherwise, my Nana will make you wear so many layers of Papa's shirts and socks that we won't even be able to fit inside the tent." Then Robyn told them how Nana had overdressed her for outdoor camping the night before last. The girls thought her story was comical.

"Did you have a happy Thanksgiving?" J.J. asked Robyn.

At first, she thought about announcing her big news about the baby, but she decided to wait. Since her talk on Stone Mountain with Papa Hart and Uncle Steve, Robyn was feeling a little better about the baby coming. But still, she wanted to keep the news to herself a while longer, and let it sink into her heart. "Yes, we ate too much. How about you?"

J.J. said that Grandmother Teresa made fry bread

and honey and roasted corn in the husks on an open fire to go with their Thanksgiving turkey.

"That sounds yummy," said Cassie. "We had turkey and ham at our house, mainly because we have such a big family. My brother, Sid, brought his girlfriend to meet us. I think he's in love."

When Cassie said "in love," she said it in a mushy, head-over-heels, love-sicky sort of way. The others laughed and remarked with "ughs" and "ichs."

Liz told them that her Thanksgiving consisted of cleaning up after her little sister the entire time. "We had a house full of guests, and my mother was so busy. So I was put in charge of Megan. It was rough. Have any of you tried to wash dried pumpkin and peas out of a four-year-old's hair before? It's impossible," she said with a dramatic sigh. "I am just only too glad to be here, gabbing with girlfriends now!"

Robyn made a mental note to talk to Liz later about little siblings, since she was about to have one herself. In the meantime, she showed them every inch of her Nana and Papa Hart's yard, including the woods out back.

They climbed a mimosa tree in a clearing with stair-step branches. For a while, they chatted in the mimosa tree, with each girl perched on her own limb like a magpie. That's when J.J. told the rest of the girls her big news.

Girl Talk

"I'm not really sure how to feel about it yet," said J.J., lowering her voice. The news was obviously very important and very private. "Yesterday I started my first period."

"Your first what?" asked Robyn.

"Shh!" said J.J.

"Your first what?" whispered Robyn.

"You know," said Cassie, "I'm sure your aunt has explained. It is something that starts happening to our growing bodies, when we get to be young ladies."

"Oh, that," said Robyn. She remembered her talk earlier with Aunt Felicia and Nana Hart about babies and how they come.

When there wasn't a baby growing in the womb, a young lady would have a menstrual period to get rid of the extra fluids that had built up inside. She certainly wasn't looking forward to having "periods" herself. In fact, she hoped it wouldn't happen for quite a while yet.

But just in case it did start happening soon, she decided to ask J.J., "Does it hurt to have a period?"

"Only a little," J.J. said, patting her middle. "I had a little bit of a tummy ache yesterday, but it's better today. Exercise helps it go away."

Robyn crossed her arms and huffed. "It sounds like periods aren't periods at all. They sound more like question marks."

Cassie nearly fell off her branch laughing. "Oh, Robyn, you are too funny. It's called a period because it lasts just for a period of a few days. It's not a punctuation mark!"

"I know," said Robyn. "But I still think a question mark is a more fitting name for it, because it doesn't make any sense to me."

"I started my period this fall, too," said Liz. "My mother was ever so surprised, since I just turned ten years old. She thought I was a little young for this to start."

"You too, Liz?" Cassie seemed disappointed that she hadn't experienced a period yet. She added, "I have been waiting and expecting to start my period for a few months now, but it hasn't happened yet."

"Why would you *want* to have it?" asked Robyn in awe.

Cassie shrugged and smiled. "I guess because I have two older sisters, and I want to be grown up like them. It's just a natural thing that happens. It first happened to Pat and Greta when they were each ten-and-a-half. I'm eleven now, so my mom and sisters think it will happen to me soon."

Just then J.J. gasped. "Oh no!" she exclaimed. "I forgot to bring my supplies with me! Robyn, do you think that your Nana might have some pads inside that I could use while I'm here?"

"Maybe," said Robyn. "We can ask."

Girl Talk

She felt sorry for J.J., having to worry about such things. It didn't sound like any fun to her at all. It didn't seem fair. Nothing like this ever happened to boys—and why not? Suddenly, Robyn felt slightly annoyed with her pals Iggy Potts and Hunter Harris for no good reason at all. All the same, they weren't burdened by being girls and having to suffer through these monthly experiences. *Boys,* Robyn thought, *have it way too easy.*

Girl Talk

10

Just then Liz's branch began to creak and crack. In a sudden fit of laughter, they all decided it might be best to climb out of the tree before they fell out! One by one, they scrambled to the ground.

"I guess we're growing up in more ways than one," said J.J., dusting her hands off on her jeans. "Maybe we're too big now to be climbing trees."

"I'll never stop climbing trees," said Robyn. "In fact, when I'm as old as my neighbor, Mrs. Snow, I'm going to keep climbing trees."

"You might look a little funny," said Cassie, giggling. "Can't you just see Robyn as an old lady, hanging from a tree branch?"

"Yes, I can," laughed Liz, as she tossed her blonde ponytail.

Robyn had to admit that it did sound a little eccentric. But just because she would be grown up someday, she didn't want to have to give up the fun things she got to do as a girl.

"Whatever floats your boat!" exclaimed J.J.

The girls went inside and found Nana Hart. Robyn whispered in Nana's ear. Nana's eyes widened and she said, "No, why do you need them?"

Robyn whispered again.

"Oh," said Nana, smiling at J.J. "Well, dears, I have to go to the pharmacy anyway for your Aunt Felicia's vitamins. So why don't you just come along with me? We can pick up what J.J. needs."

"Thank you, Mrs. Hart," said J.J.

"Oh, call me Nana if you like!"

"Thank you, Nana!" exclaimed J.J. After that, all Robyn's guests called her grandparents Nana and Papa Hart, just like her. It pleased Robyn to no end.

On the way to the pharmacy, Robyn asked Liz what it was like having a little sister. She didn't expect the answer she got!

"Well," said Liz matter-of-factly, "she is a human squirrel. She stores things away in the strangest places! This morning I found a plate of dried up apple pieces in the coat closet. Who knows how long it had been there? Maybe weeks!"

"And your mother makes you clean up after her?" asked Robyn. Secretly she wondered if Aunt Felicia would have such high expectations of her.

"Sometimes," said Liz. "My mom and dad are under a lot of stress right now, so I have to help out. My little sister is a handful. She cries if she doesn't get things her way."

"Oh," said Robyn. So far, this sister stuff wasn't sounding like a bit of fun.

"But there are times when we get along great," said Liz.

"There are?" Robyn asked hopefully.

"Oh sure," said Liz, with a mischievous look on her face. "When she's asleep, for example." Cassie and J.J. laughed, but Robyn did not. "But I love my little sister, and I wouldn't trade her for anything. However, if anyone wants to *borrow* her once in a while, let me know!"

Before they knew it, they had arrived at the pharmacy. The girls were simply amazed at the wide selection of sanitary supplies that were available on the shelf.

"Which kind do you need?" asked Robyn, confused by all the descriptions on the boxes. Words like *wings* and *flaps* were confusing to Robyn.

Finally, J.J. found the kind she needed. They were made in a special slender size for young ladies.

Next, they headed to the checkout line, where J.J. paid with her own pocket money. Robyn was waiting for her by the bubble gum dispenser when she realized something. She and her friends were growing up fast—too fast for comfort. Even at this very moment, changes were taking place. Would they all really be *women* someday soon?

Robyn, who usually felt proud of being grown up and independent, suddenly wasn't comfortable with leaving her childhood behind at all. She looked down and was glad to see that her chest was still flat, at least for the time being. J.J. and Liz were both noticeably "blossoming."

Unlike Cassie, Robyn preferred to stay just as she was, at least for a while longer. But she knew that time was going to keep changing her friends and herself. She felt as if her childhood was fleeting, and there was nothing much that she could do about it.

By nightfall, Liz, Cassie, and J.J. were all asking Robyn, "Is anything wrong?"

"No, of course not, why?" Robyn replied for the umpteenth time.

"You're being awfully quiet," said Liz, as they slipped on their pajamas, just after nightfall.

Robyn shrugged. "Oh, I guess there are some things on my mind."

"Well, it's not good to keep your worries inside," said Cassie. "Why don't you tell us what you're thinking about? Maybe we can help."

"That's what friends are for!" added J.J., as she slipped on her footie-socks with a different color for every toe.

Robyn smiled. "It's kind of a secret. But tonight, once we're settled down in the tent under the twinkle lights and the stars, I'll tell you," she promised.

Just then, there was a knock at the guest room door, where they had been changing into their pajamas. "Come in," the four sang in unison.

Aunt Felicia entered the room and smiled at the sight she saw. There were four girls snug in their warmest pajamas. Around them, there appeared to have been an unusual storm. Socks and shoes, jeans, and tops had rained down all over the place. There were also hairbrushes, toothbrushes, bracelets, school pictures of friends, barrettes, and ponytail holders.

"My goodness," said Aunt Felicia. "Slumber parties are so much fun, but very messy. How about if each of you collects your belongings before you head outside to the tent? Here, I'll help you."

"Sorry," said J.J., "we just got excited about camping and totally forgot about being neat and orderly."

"I remember those days, when all my friends would pile in together," said Aunt Felicia. "Robyn's mother and I had some great slumber parties here in this very room, when we were growing into young women. They are wonderful memories to treasure for a lifetime."

Pretty soon, the room was back in order. Four stacks of clothing and shoes and accessories were neatly lined up along the dresser top.

"All right, tent, here I come!" exclaimed Cassie, and she took off with her CD player.

Liz hollered, "I'm right behind you!"

Then J.J. scampered out, calling, "Good night!"

Aunt Felicia looked into Robyn's eyes and asked her, "Are you feeling all right, baby bird?"

"Yes, thank you," said Robyn, wishing her feelings weren't so obvious to everyone. "I'm still getting used to our baby news. And it seems like we—my friends and I—are changing too. I thought I wanted to be grown up, but now I'm not so sure. We aren't going to be plain little girls much longer, are we?"

Aunt Felicia smiled. "Oh, I see. Yes, I think the ages of ten, eleven, and twelve are some of the most confusing years. On one hand, you don't feel like playing the same childhood games anymore. But on the other hand, you're not quite ready for the role of being a young woman, either."

"How did you know?" Robyn asked, amazed. Aunt Felicia understood exactly how she felt.

"Oh, believe me, I remember how I felt at your age," said Aunt Felicia. "One minute, I would want to grow up and go to a party with my older sister—your mother—and her friends, yet I liked resting in the security of knowing I was my daddy's little girl. It was a very challenging time for me and for my parents!"

"I think J.J. is more ready to grow up than I am," said Robyn, a little sulkily.

"I suppose that's true. After all, J.J. is older than you are," Aunt Felicia noted. "Don't worry, when the time comes, you'll be ready to grow up. You have already grown up so much."

"Do you really think so?"

"I know so. But remember, you don't have to be like anyone else to feel accepted. God made you a very special young lady, Robyn Alexa Morgan. And that is something to celebrate!" Aunt Felicia kissed her forehead. "Now, you skedaddle! Have a good night!"

Robyn smiled and grabbed her favorite teddy bear, Patch, and headed for the tent. It was a little cooler than the other night, when Robyn and her grandparents tried out the tent for the first time. But with the girls snuggling into their sleeping bags like caterpillars in cocoons, the close quarters were quite cozy and warm. Side by side, from left to right were Cassie, Liz, Robyn, and J.J.

Giggling girls, upbeat music on the CD player, and the twinkle lights made the tent feel extra-festive. Soon after she had nestled into her sleeping bag, Robyn crawled out again to open the moon roof flap. That way, the girls could lie on their backs and count the stars.

When they had grown tired of the CD they had played through twice, Cassie hit the stop button. For a while, they listened to the crickets, which were still making late autumn songs in the woods with their tiny, spindle legs.

Then J.J. asked, "Say Robyn, when are you going to share your secret with us?"

Adventures in Misty Falls

A star that flickered like a blue diamond caught Robyn's eye. She held her breath for a moment, wondering if the time was right to tell. She decided that now was as good a time as any. "Aunt Felicia is expecting a baby in February or March."

A chorus of squeals emitted from the tent, as the girls celebrated the joyful news. "How exciting!" exclaimed Cassie. "Congratulations, Robyn."

"Thanks," said Robyn, "I think."

"What's the matter," J.J. asked, "aren't you happy about it?"

Robyn told them she was happy for Uncle Steve and Aunt Felicia, but she was a little unsure about being a big sister.

"Oh Robyn, I hope it isn't because of what I said about my little sister, Megan," said Liz, who sat bolt upright inside her sleeping bag. "I didn't mean to discourage you. Being a big sister does have its good points too, you know."

"Thanks, Liz, and don't worry," said Robyn. "You didn't discourage me. I think I'll be fine about the baby, once I get used to the idea."

"Sure you will," said J.J. "I have an idea. When your aunt is busy in the Pet Cottage, I'll come over and help you take care of the new baby."

"I'll help too," said Cassie. "I love little babies."

Liz piped up. "Maybe we could go to the park with my little sister and your little brother or sister, Robyn.

Do you know if the baby is a boy or a girl?"

"Not yet," said Robyn. "Thanks, you all. Maybe being a big sister is going to be fun."

"Of course it will," said Cassie. "I'm guessing though, since I'm the baby in my family!"

"Do you feel better now?" asked J.J., patting Robyn's arm.

"Yes, I guess so," said Robyn. "But I think my mixed-up feelings are about more than just the baby. But before I say anything else, do you all promise that nothing we say goes outside this tent?"

"Promise!" said Liz, Cassie, and J.J.

"Okay," said Robyn. She sat up in her sleeping bag and lowered her voice. "Do any of you ever get the feeling we are stuck between being little girls and being grown-up young ladies?"

"YES!" exclaimed Cassie.

"Absolutely," said J.J.

"You can say *that* again!" said Liz.

Then they all started talking at once and got tickled at each other. "You go first, Liz," said Cassie.

"Okay," said Liz. "This might sound kind of silly to you all . . . ."

"No, go ahead," said Robyn. She was glad someone else besides her was feeling a little awkward.

"Well, I've recently had to start wearing a grown-up kind of bra, and I feel embarrassed at school. Most of the other girls in fifth grade haven't filled out as much as I have. I feel different," said Liz. "Sometimes I just want my body to be the way it used to be."

Robyn's heart went out to Liz. That would be a terrible predicament to find oneself in. She knew how much the boys liked to tease her about her limp. She couldn't imagine the ribbing that Liz probably took about her changing body. In Robyn's opinion, that would be even worse!

"Oh, Liz," said Cassie, "You should feel very good about yourself. You are such a pretty girl. My mom would probably tell you one of her favorite Scripture verses if she were here—oh something like, 'you are fearfully and wonderfully made.' "

"Thank you, Cassie," said Liz. "Sometimes I feel like I don't fit in."

"Me too," said Cassie and J.J. together.

"Me too!" said Robyn, with surprise. "Wow, if all four of us feel awkward about ourselves sometimes, don't you suppose everybody does?"

"Probably," said Cassie, giggling. "I was always embarrassed about having these little prickly bumps on my skin. My doctor says they will disappear as I grow up. So I would just like to get older fast and have clear skin! If I could, I would want to trade in my skin for J.J.'s."

Everyone agreed that J.J.'s beautiful bronze complexion was perfect. She was such a pretty young lady.

"Thank you," said J.J., "but do you know what?

Girl Talk

Sometimes I don't know whether I want to get one more day older. I mean, what will I do with myself when I don't feel like doing kid things anymore? It's kind of silly, but once in a while I like to get out my Barbie dolls—or even paper dolls. Other times, I feel funny playing with them. Sometimes, I think I should pack them up and put them in the attic. Especially now that I've started to have a period like older girls."

Robyn knew exactly what the attachment to favorite toys like dolls felt like. Here she was, sitting in the tent holding onto Patch, her faithful teddy from her childhood. Patch had been through every surgery with her since the car accident when she was three years old.

Maybe that was why she couldn't even think about putting Patch in a box in the attic. Robyn secretly supposed that even when she was twenty, she would still be sleeping with her teddy bear every night. It made her giggle to think of such a thing, but it was probably true!

"Oh well," giggled Cassie, "at least we don't still suck our thumbs!" Then she thought a moment and added, "Do we?"

All the girls burst into a fit of silly giggles. Robyn sucked her thumb for fun and said, "So what if we do?" It felt good to feel so close to her friends tonight in the tent. She felt free. Her friends were allowing her to be herself, and that felt wonderful.

They all settled down on their backs and looked at the stars again. Robyn was sure that if she were still for five seconds, she would be sound asleep. But it wasn't to be.

Instead, Liz's stomach began to make the most interesting noises. "I think I'm hungry!" she announced.

That produced another fit of laughter, and the girls sat up again. Robyn pulled out the treats Nana had packed for them. By twinkle light, the girls opened the package of vanilla wafers and spread peanut butter on them. Then they needed something to drink, so Robyn and Cassie were assigned the job of sneaking into the house for four cups of cold milk.

There was something unusually amusing about four girls gobbling cookies and milk in the middle of the night, when the rest of the world was sleeping. Robyn had never laughed so much in her life, to the point that she snorted milk out her nostrils by accident. One thing was certain, she was still very much a girl and not a young lady in the least. And for tonight, that was just fine with Robyn!

Girl Talk

11

The next day dawned a little too early for four sleepy girls who had stayed up too late. Nevertheless, they emerged from their brief slumber with yawns and stretches.

J.J. shook the cookie crumbs out of her sleeping bag and rolled it up. But Robyn, Cassie, and Liz were far too tired to take the time to do such a thing.

Since Uncle Steve was heading to the mall to work for half a day, he offered to take the girls and Aunt Felicia with him. "Lots of Christmas sales are starting today," he had hinted, "and I have my wish list ready!"

The word *Christmas* was enough to wake up Robyn and her friends. They hurried through showers and were ready to go when Uncle Steve called them to the car.

At the mall, Robyn was amazed at how many people were there to buy Christmas presents ... all because God's Baby Son was born in a cow's feeding trough over 2000 years ago in a tiny town called Bethlehem.

Everywhere they looked, there were bright-colored Christmas decorations, Santas, elves, and every Christmas present imaginable for everyone in Robyn's family. But to her disappointment, Aunt Felicia ended up shopping for maternity clothes.

Clothes for expectant mothers were not very exciting for Robyn and her friends. Especially when there were earrings and necklaces and games and puzzles and CDs and sports equipment throughout the mall. It wasn't that she didn't want Aunt Felicia to have nice clothes to wear while she was pregnant, but such items weren't among Robyn's top ten things to shop for.

Matters got worse from there. As they were passing through the undergarments department, Aunt Felicia took Robyn aside and whispered, "I noticed that all your friends are wearing bras now. You're growing up, dear Robyn. Perhaps we should purchase your first bra while we are here."

Robyn blushed a shade of purple at the very thought. It might be kind of nice to be like her friends, but on the other hand, she wasn't sure she wanted that tight binding around her chest.

J.J. overheard Aunt Felicia talking to Robyn. She encouraged her younger friend to try one on. So with the clerk's help, Robyn was fitted for her first training bra. The other girls waited outside the dressing room, until Aunt Felicia said, "We'll take it. She can wear it home today."

While Aunt Felicia went to the cash register, Robyn came out of the dressing room, tugging at the new article of clothing she wore under her blouse. "Am I still blushing?" she asked a little miserably.

"Yes," said Cassie. "Oh, Robyn, don't feel self-conscious. You look very nice and perfectly natural."

J.J. and Liz agreed. "Now we are alike," J.J. said, trying to make Robyn feel better.

Robyn felt pretty silly walking around the mall wearing something strangely new to her. But after a while, she forgot all about it. . .that is, until the girls ran into Iggy Potts and Hunter Harris at the cookie shop.

Robyn reasoned that the boys would have no way of knowing about her new purchase. Still, she felt embarrassed to see them, as if they might read her mind and think it a good reason to tease her.

She should have known better, though. Iggy and Hunter had never teased to be mean or rude. They were very polite friends, and Robyn decided it would be better if she forgot all about her new article of clothing. So they all bought cookies and sat around a nearby table and talked, until the boys had to go home with Hunter's parents.

That afternoon, Uncle Steve took the girls back to

Nana's house. While Aunt Felicia modeled her new maternity dress for Nana, Papa, and Uncle Steve, the girls modeled old prom dresses that had belonged to Aunt Felicia and Robyn's mother when they were in high school and college. It was fun playing dress-up with real sparkling gowns! Nana, Papa, Uncle Steve, and Aunt Felicia made a receptive audience for the girls' modeling show.

That's when J.J. said they would look just like real ladies with a little lipstick. So Nana hopped up and took them to her room. She helped them apply their very first makeup. Aunt Felicia objected, but Nana said it was okay to let the girls try some lipstick and powder, since they were dressed in such fine evening wear.

"Just this once won't hurt," said Nana.

Aunt Felicia sighed. "These girls are children, Mother. Don't put ideas into their heads."

"Too late, Aunt Felicia," said Robyn, as Nana finished helping her apply Passion Pink to her lips. "How do I look?"

"Like a clown," said Liz, bursting into fits of laughter. Her own Raving Ruby lips were too bright for words.

"Like a clown is right," said Aunt Felicia, frowning. "Let's wait a few years for the makeup, girls. All right?"

It was just like a grandmother to let little girls get by with extra mischief, and Robyn was glad that Nana had "won" today's argument. True, none of the girls was ready to wear cosmetics "for real." But it was fun to try it and pretend to be older for just a little while.

Then Aunt Felicia insisted that it was time to wash their faces. The girls didn't argue, so they lined up at the bathroom sink for a good scrubbing. Afterward, Aunt Felicia polished their fingernails and told them not to grow up too fast and to enjoy being young as long as they could. The girls promised to do just that!

That evening after supper, they were heading outside to sleep in the tent, but Nana stopped them. "The weather is turning much colder tonight. Maybe you had better sleep in the guest room," she advised.

"Oh no!" objected Robyn. She had really wanted one more night in the tent. "Can't we please sleep in the tent?"

"I'm afraid you'll all catch cold," said Nana. "But we can make a tent here in the den for you."

So they followed Nana to the closet and pulled out three of the biggest blankets they could find. Then they spread them over the tops of the couch, recliner, and tables to make a tent. Nana and Papa attached the blankets so their "roof" wouldn't fall down in the night. Cassie and J.J. went out to retrieve the sleeping bags from the tent and came in shivering.

"Your Nana is right," said J.J. "It's really getting cold out there!"

Robyn and Liz found some old flashlights in Papa's workshop and a big box of photographs of Robyn in the garage. Most of the photographs were from her baby days. Then inside their makeshift inside tent, Cassie, J.J., and Liz oohed and aahed over the baby faces in the pictures, until Robyn put a lid on the box and said, "That's enough of that!"

Aunt Felicia showed the girls a special box of dolls and doll clothes from her own childhood. They dressed the dolls, which had been wrapped in plastic bags to protect them from the dampness. The dolls were sweet-faced and had eyes that opened and closed.

Sitting in the floor next to them, Aunt Felicia told them about her favorite doll of all. "This is Betsy," she said affectionately, holding Betsy in her arms like a real baby. "She really wets, and if you hold her up to your ear, she will tell you that she loves you. At least, that's what I always imagined. I slept with her every night for years."

"How did you give up sleeping with her?" asked Robyn. "I mean, when did you decide to put her away in the box?"

"One night Nana came to tuck me in as usual," Robyn's aunt remembered. "She said that Betsy and I were growing up. She said she wondered if Betsy would like to sleep in her blanket on my dresser, instead of with me in my bed. I said I supposed that would be all right, as long as I could see Betsy from my bed and get her if she started to cry."

"And did she cry?" asked Liz intently.

"No, she didn't," said Aunt Felicia. "I listened for her for at least an hour. I couldn't sleep without her for a while, but finally we both drifted off to sleep. The next morning, I put Betsy in her high chair and fed her breakfast. As time went on, I played with her a little less every day. Eventually, she ended up in the box in the attic. She's still my favorite doll, though. And I always have a special place in my heart for her."

"Just like I do for Patch," said Robyn, reaching for her teddy bear. "How old were you when you stopped sleeping with Betsy, Aunt Felicia?"

"I think I was nine or ten," she said. "But I'm not sure. It was a long time ago! But I still remember what it was like to have a favorite doll."

When Aunt Felicia had kissed them all on their foreheads, she woke up Uncle Steve, who had fallen asleep on the floor beside her. Off they went to bed. Papa and Nana had already retired for the evening.

Now was Robyn's favorite time with friends…the time when the whole house was asleep except the late-night gigglers. Until they grew too sleepy to play, Robyn dealt Old Maid cards, but they weren't just any Old Maid cards. They were cards from the late 1950s that Nana had saved for Robyn to play with.

Not a card had been lost in all those years, and it was much more fun to play with cards that had comical people on them named "Pickle Face Pittman," "Blabbermouth Betty," and "Handy Hiram Hovater." The only thing was, Robyn knew every crease in the Old Maid card. Even though she tried not to notice, she always knew who was holding the Old Maid. But the other girls didn't seem to care. They were too busy catching the silly giggles again, anyway.

As they finally settled into their sleeping bags and grew quieter, Liz whispered, "I'm sorry this is our last night before we go home. I like it better here than at my house. Nobody gets mad at each other here."

"What do you mean, Liz?" asked Robyn, suddenly wide-eyed again.

"Oh, I don't know. I guess my mom and dad argue sometimes when I am trying to fall asleep at night. It makes it hard to relax," she explained.

For a moment, the girls were silent. Robyn reached over and patted Liz's hand.

Then Cassie piped up. "We should make a promise to each other...that we'll be each other's sisters anytime one of us needs help or needs a good listener."

"Good idea!" agreed J.J. "In *Little Women* by Louisa May Alcott, Meg and Jo looked out for their little sisters all the time. Meg took Amy under her wing, and Jo took care of Beth. Robyn, would you and Liz like for Cassie and me to be your big sisters?"

"Yes!" said Robyn excitedly.

Cassie suggested that she and Liz become sisters, and that Robyn and J.J. team up. That was just what they did. And to make sure they did this "sister thing" right, they all agreed to read *Little Women* between now and Christmas.

"That makes me feel better," said Liz. "Thanks, Cassie, for being my sister."

"Remember, we're all sisters," said J.J. "As we grow up together, we will never have to face anything without each other."

At that, Robyn smiled and fell soundly asleep.

Girl Talk

12

The next morning, four bright-eyed girls met Nana in the kitchen. But Nana looked so troubled, that Robyn knew instantly something was wrong.

"It's Aunt Felicia," said Nana. "It's probably nothing to worry about, but Uncle Steve took her to the hospital in the night. She was having a few uncomfortable pains. We called the doctor and he said he wanted to look at her and make sure she and the baby are all right."

Robyn wanted to go to the hospital right away to be with Aunt Felicia and Uncle Steve. She felt a little guilty that she hadn't been excited about the baby when she was told on Thanksgiving Day. Now, what if something happened to Aunt Felicia or the baby—or both?

But Nana reassured her. "Oh, there now, darling, it isn't your fault! Everything is probably all right," she said. "Let's have some breakfast and then we'll take your friends home and go by the hospital."

Around the table, the girls and Nana held hands as Papa prayed for God's protection. Robyn could hardly swallow her oatmeal. All she wanted to do was be with Aunt Felicia. *Was her aunt afraid? Was the baby going to be born too early?*

There was nothing to do but get ready to go. The girls packed in silence and hurried to the car after breakfast. They knew that Robyn, Nana, and Papa Hart needed to be with Aunt Felicia as soon as they could. Robyn appreciated her friends—her new sisters—all the more for their understanding.

Even though they weren't talking very much to each other, there was unspoken tender loving care among them. Robyn was glad they had spent the last couple of days together.

All the way to Misty Falls, over and over, Robyn prayed, "Lord, please be with Aunt Felicia and the baby."

Papa dropped off Cassie and J.J. off at J.J.'s house, and then took Liz home. Then he drove to the hospital. *If only we had a siren on our car like an ambulance,* Robyn thought to herself. That way, they could move faster through traffic. But she had to be patient and just wait.

Trying to find a parking place at the hospital was practically impossible, but Papa finally found a space a block away. Robyn tried to keep up with Papa's long, anxious steps down the sidewalk and up to the hospital. The familiar sterile smell of the hospital filled Robyn with dread. She kept praying silently to God as they walked to the information counter.

There, a nice lady made a few phone calls and directed them to the right place. Aunt Felicia had been seen in the emergency room, she said, and they had just taken her upstairs to labor and delivery.

Robyn's mouth flew open. *That was the place where babies were born, wasn't it? But it wasn't nearly time for Aunt Felicia's baby to be born . . . .*

Nana's mouth had pursed with tension as they made their way up the elevator to the second floor. Robyn had many questions flying through her head, but she decided not to ask anything just now. She had never seen Papa and Nana look so concerned.

As soon as they stepped off the elevator, Robyn could hear newborn babies crying. Everything on the floor was painted pink or blue, and the bulletin board had been decorated with baby rattles, bottles, and tiny little diapers with the message, "New Mommies and Daddies Class Every Tuesday and Saturday at 7:00 P.M. Sign up at the Nurse's Desk." Robyn hoped that Aunt Felicia and Uncle Steve would get to take that class someday.

At the nurse's desk, Papa asked about Felicia Hart Morgan. "She's in the room right across the hall, sir," said the head nurse. "You may go in for just a moment. The doctor will be checking her shortly."

Adventures in Misty Falls

Whisk! Robyn followed Papa and Nana into the
room. There was Uncle Steve standing with his back
to them and facing a bed. Aunt Felicia was in the bed
with a sheet over her. "Hi, family," said Aunt Felicia
with a weak smile.

"Are you all right, dear?" asked Nana, practically in
tears.

"Yes, I'm all right. How's my baby bird?"

Robyn bent over to kiss Aunt Felicia on the forehead. "The question is," said Robyn, "how are you
and the baby?"

"Well," said Aunt Felicia, "I think we are both going
to be fine. They are wondering why my abdomen has
grown so much and why I am in such discomfort.
The doctor is coming around in a little while to do an
ultrasound test."

"What's that?" asked Robyn.

"He will put some gel on my tummy and place
something that looks like a computer mouse over it.
It will pick up signals from the baby and put an
image of the baby on this TV screen over here."

"Oh," said Robyn, feeling anxious. "Aunt Felicia,
I'm used to being the one sick in bed, not you. Please
get well."

"Don't worry, baby bird," said Aunt Felicia calmly.
"This is just a checkup."

Just then the nurse came into the room. "You'll all
need to wait in the waiting room, please. The doctor

is on his way. Mr. Morgan, you may stay with your wife."

Papa, Nana, and Robyn waved good-bye and went to wait in the room at the end of the hall. Reading magazines at a time like this was just impossible. Sitting still was also impossible. Robyn felt like tap-dancing her jitters away, but that made Papa nervous. So she tried very hard to remain calm, until—until what? Robyn didn't know.

After what seemed like hours, the head nurse came in to talk to Papa and Nana. "Your daughter is fine and just needs bed rest," she said.

"Thank the good Lord," said Nana, looking heaven-ward. "What about the baby?"

"The doctor would like to invite you all to come in to see the ultrasound pictures. Is this the Morgans' daughter?" the nurse asked, looking at Robyn.

"Yes, this is their daughter," said Nana, smiling into Robyn's eyes.

"Then she may come too," said the nurse.

Robyn couldn't wait to skip into Aunt Felicia's room. She dashed ahead of the nurse and her grand-parents. When she entered, Uncle Steve looked like he had seen a ghost. He was sitting in a chair in the corner, with his head down between his knees. What Robyn could see of his face was all pale and sweaty.

"Uncle Steve, maybe you ought to be the one to lie down," said Robyn. "Are you all right?"

"He's just having some fatherly jitters," said the doctor kindly. "And for good reason. If you will all take a look on the monitor here, we're going to visit Felicia's womb and see what we can see."

Aunt Felicia's eyes were glued to the monitor, and her mouth was open in awe of the miracle on the screen. What looked like a photocopy of a baby with little eyes, nose, and ears was on the screen. It was moving around. Robyn could see it! It was waving at her!

"OH!" said Aunt Felicia and Nana together. Papa chuckled at the sight of his newest grandchild. Robyn grinned. That was her little brother or sister!

Dr. Cathcart smiled and said, "It's a healthy one, but from this angle I can't quite tell if it is a boy or a girl."

"Goodie! Our baby is fine!" exclaimed Robyn. Then she had another thought. "But Doctor, why is Aunt Felicia hurting if everything is okay?"

"Well now, good question, young lady," replied Dr. Cathcart. "You see, when I move over to this side of the womb, we find that our little resident has a room-mate!"

Robyn looked back at the monitor. Dr. Cathcart moved the "mouse" over Aunt Felicia's swollen tummy to the other side. There, next to the baby was—another baby! A little baby with ten fingers and ten toes, little eyes, ears, and a button nose. This one was sucking its tiny little thumb!

Girl Talk

Robyn exclaimed, "Oh my goodness! TWINS! Aunt Felicia, we're going to have twins!"

Now Papa and Nana had to sit down next to Uncle Steve. But Robyn laughed and hugged Aunt Felicia tightly. "We're going to have our hands full, aren't we?" said Aunt Felicia joyfully.

Dr. Cathcart turned off the monitor. Then he listened to the babies' heartbeats. *Whoo-whooo-whooo-whooo* went the sound of two tiny hearts beating out a cadence over the speaker. This was a miracle!

Aunt Felicia asked, "So everything is perfectly okay with the babies?"

"Yes, they are as healthy as can be," he said. "However, the discomfort you felt earlier was little involuntary muscle contractions. We want to stop them by putting you to bed for a week or two. It's important for you to keep the babies inside the womb for a few more months. We can do that if you will get plenty of bed rest and take the prescription that I'm going to give you."

"All right, thank you, Dr. Cathcart," said Aunt Felicia gratefully.

Then Dr. Cathcart turned to Uncle Steve, Nana, and Papa. "We'll keep her here for observation today and tonight. Then if all goes as we expect, she can go home tomorrow."

Uncle Steve stood and shook hands with the doctor. Then he kissed Aunt Felicia. "Well, Little Mama," he said, "how does it feel to know you're going to give birth to twins in a few months?"

"Totally amazing," said Aunt Felicia. "I'm so excited. And there's so much to do to get ready! Oh, Steve, but if I have to rest all the time, who will get the nursery ready?"

Uncle Steve looked at Robyn. Robyn looked at Uncle Steve. "We can paint," said Robyn.

Then Nana chimed in, "I can make curtains and matching sheets and pillows for the nursery."

"I can find matching cribs and take care of my girl," said Papa, winking at Aunt Felicia.

Happy tears filled Aunt Felicia's dark eyes. "You all are such a terrific family. Thank you," she said.

Robyn stayed with Aunt Felicia while everyone else went downstairs for a cup of coffee in the cafeteria. Suddenly, Robyn realized something very amazing as she thought back over the last few moments. As soon as she had seen the babies on the ultrasound monitor, God had filled her heart with love for them!

Besides, Aunt Felicia needed her now more than ever, and she would help in every way she could. "Don't worry about anything, Aunt Felicia," she said with a big smile. "Just rest."

"You're the best, baby bird," said Aunt Felicia with her eyes half closed. Then she breathed a long, happy sigh. "It's such a miracle to see our babies on the TV monitor, isn't it?"

"Yes," said Robyn. "I didn't expect to get to see my little brothers or sisters. By the way . . . ."

"What?"

"Was I as little as those babies when I was in my mother's womb?" asked Robyn.

"Definitely," said Aunt Felicia.

Robyn smiled. "Now I belong to you and Uncle Steve. If I'm the babies' big sister, do you suppose they might grow up wondering why I'm calling their mother 'Aunt Felicia'?"

"Now that's something I hadn't thought of," said Aunt Felicia.

"Would you mind if I were to call you Mama from now on?" Robyn asked a little shyly.

"Nothing would please me more, baby bird," came the soft answer. "That is, if it is comfortable for you."

"You are my mother in all the ways that really count," said Robyn. "And today, God has made me glad and proud to be a big sister."

"You will be a wonderful big sister, and you're a daughter to be proud of."

Robyn felt truly blessed and thankful for the first time in a while...thankful to be growing up at her own special pace, thankful for the opportunity to be a big sister, and thankful for a loving family and caring sister-friends like Cassie, J.J., and Liz.

Robyn grinned as she said, "Liz clued me in that little siblings make lots of baby messes. So just in case

you're wondering, Mama, I'll be glad to help you
clean up after our twins. After all, what's a big sister
for?"

Address: ▼ http://www.mistyfallsfriends.com

Back　Forward　Stop　Refresh　Home　Search　Mail　Favorites

A WHOLE NEW MISTY FALLS WORLD IS READY FOR YOU TO EXPLORE ON THE WEB!

What do Cassie and the gang do in their spare time?

What games do they like to play?

What's going on at Misty Falls Middle School?

What does Misty Falls look like?

**Visit
www.mistyfallsfriends.com
to find out!**

Don't miss any of the adventures of Cassie and the Misty Falls gang.

Read all the books!

 ☐ **Cassie, You're a Winner!**
1-56309-735-4
N007116
$4.99 retail price
$2.99 through
12/31/01

 ☐ **Robyn to the Rescue**
1-56309-451-7
N007109
$4.99

 ☐ **Best Friends Forever?**
1-56309-734-6
N007117
$4.99

 ☐ **Tell the Truth, Cassie**
1-56309-452-5
N007110
$4.99

 ☐ **J.J., Navajo Princess**
1-56309-763-X
N007105
$4.99

 ☐ **Girl Talk**
1-56309-455-X
N017103
$4.99

 ☐ **Robyn Flies Home**
1-56309-764-8
N007106
$4.99

 ☐ **Way Too Cool**
1-56309-456-8
N017104
$4.99

Look for books 9 and 10—available in 2002!